A.A. Balaskovits

Magic for unlucky Girls

sf**WP**)

sfwp.com

Library of Congress Cataloging-in-Publication Data

Names: Balaskovits, A. A., author.
Title: Magic for unlucky girls : stories / A.A. Balaskovits.
Description: Santa Fe, NM : SFWP, [2017] | Includes bibliographical
  references and index.
Identifiers: LCCN 2016033041 (print) | LCCN 2016039274 (ebook) |
  ISBN 9781939650665 (trade paper : alk. paper) | ISBN 9781939650672 (pdf) |
  ISBN 9781939650689 (epub) | ISBN 9781939650696 (mobi)
Subjects: LCSH: Girls—Fiction. | Fairy tales—Adaptations.
Classification: LCC PS3602.A594 M34 2017 (print) | LCC PS3602.A594 (ebook) |
  DDC 813/.6—dc23
LC record available at https://lccn.loc.gov/2016033041

Published by SFWP
369 Montezuma Ave. #350
Santa Fe, NM 87501
(505) 428-9045
www.sfwp.com

Find the author at www.aabalaskovits.com

Cover art: Arthur Rackham, "Goblin Market"

For my Mother and my Father

contents

Put Back together Again

t was July when I first saw him, a hot July, the kind of July that you remember because you spent the whole month drenched, and you were amazed that your body could stand to lose all its water. We all looked to the sky. The devout clasped their hands. That month I kept a tally of gunshot wounds blaring into the ER. During the winter, when it's too cold to set a pinky out the door, people keep their guns in shoeboxes and use kitchen knives. Then they roll bloody out of ambulances. The bodies come in on their backs or their sides, porcelain and metal handles sticking out from their skin like deformed arms. The whole city was at the mercy of the weather, blandly dictating how we would mutilate one another that season.

Lizzy told me that, before med school, she used to spend her weekends chasing ambulances. There was something wrong with her blood, I suppose, because she said the noise made everything inside of her bounce and sing. Lizzy, I told her, blood always moves. It doesn't know how to stop until it stops. She was mesmerized by the red and white blinding lights, the sirens that left a trail of yelping dogs in their wake. Someone, a teacher I think, told me that sirens were made a particular pitch, one that made dogs, no matter how many times they heard it, into frightened little pups, barking mad for their mothers.

With the heat came the earthquakes—low, rumbling earth beneath the concrete. The ambulances were going off all the time now, and even a minor shake would send people into the ER, holding their heads or arms or legs from where they had hit themselves against their coffee tables, or each other. Even in the mad noise, it is easy to be bored, just something else to grow accustomed to when you hear it all the time.

That's how I knew he was not a man, not like everyone wanted him to be; the sirens still made him whimper and turn his head.

* * *

Men who dream cities dream stability, a kind of urban grace. When they planned their skyscrapers, they circled the part of the coast they would build on. They did not know it was a fault zone, which I suppose was no fault of their own. Their desire was pure in those early stages. Who could have blamed them for continuing on even as the ground began to groan and thrash? They built on sick ground; they could not see deformity for soil.

They planned where each building would go, down to excruciating detail. In the city museum, behind glass, you can see their blueprints and all the smudges and erasure marks where they could not decide what should go at its core. In black, thick letters they eventually decided on St. Ruth's, our trauma center. She stood above the others, and on its sides the other buildings decreased in size, like a glass and steel pyramid.

* * *

There were too many people in the ER the first day I saw him. There are always too many in the ER, a whole bunch of humpty-dumptys. That's what Lizzy called them, the men and women and children who were broken beyond repair but still crawled to the doors asking for help, expecting help, growing angry when they were beyond medical help. Lizzy used the same expression for the people she dated—some you hump once or twice, and some you kept around a little longer before they were sent off to the dump.

Some of the hump-dumps in the waiting room would have been better off on their own with glue and bandages, but they trusted the glue and bandages of doctors more. I gave them clipboards and pens and sent them, if they were bleeding enough, back to see the doctors. If they were only in pain, or could speak clearly, I had them sit and wait.

They came in together, a tall man with blond hair and a small woman, barely five feet tall. She was leaning on him. There was blood, dark, the kind that hits the air and congeals. She'd been bleeding for a while from her shoulder and her stomach. I knew she was a dumpty. I was shocked she could move at all and hadn't come in an ambulance, but some people just don't bother. I get that; ambulances are expensive, especially when you're just going to die anyway. It's a terrible gift to leave behind, those last bills.

The man had blood on him. He said, Sorry baby, sorry baby, sorry baby, and he was crying or sweating thick mucous all over his face.

Sir, I told him, you have to wait here. She'll be fine, I lied. I called in the codes. I said, The nurses will take her to the back. They'll care for her. You're not allowed there. Sir.

The moment the body goes from structured to diseased is a slow one, so slow you don't notice a change until it's already spread and invaded the lungs, the heart, the pancreas. Violence is not so different from disease.

The man had a gun. It should not have shocked me, but it did. When he pulled it out and aimed it at the girl, I felt disappointed and sick.

The ground rumbled beneath us, and I rumbled with it.

I thought, how did he get past the metal detectors? And then I thought that was funny.

I'm staying with her, he said.

I backed away. The humptys in the waiting area screamed and fell on the ground and covered their heads, just like we had been taught for earthquakes.

Sir, I said. Sir, calm down.

The ER nurses were staring at him. The bleeding woman was losing herself all over the floor. When this was all over they would have to disinfect everything under her. Bring in outsiders who did this sort of thing with hazmat suits. The carpet would have to be ripped out.

It'll be OK, I said. It's going to be OK.

You bitch, he said and aimed the gun at me. You're all bitches.

He shot. I heard it blast. Had it hit, the bullet would have gone through me. My face—each tiny pore, that ugly mole behind my ear, the grease and oil welled up under my eyes—would explode. There is a certain kind of intrusion that is unbearable to think of, from people who do not bother to touch you, but can make everything in you shut down. It's not like in the movies or TV where they show a clear entrance and clear exit, like a bug that burrows in and escapes with a trickle of red. When it happens, your face, or your arm or your belly, burst outward, disintegrate in the heat.

I heard the crash of my computer tumbling off my desk. I saw my papers flying around me, all those pens, the three clipboards, an empty stapler.

It did not hit me. I did not explode. A man, someone new, was in front of me. I had not seen him, not heard him. I dropped to my knees and felt my head. The man with the gun was on the ground, the ER nurses holding him down with their bodies. He was screaming and wailing on about his girl, and she was on the ground, forgotten, dying or dead.

I rolled my hands over my face. I was there.

* * *

The humptys spoke in awe to the police: the strange man had been shot, but he hadn't taken the bullet like he was supposed to. He wrestled the gunman to the floor. They fought, there was screaming, the blood from that dead girl was everywhere. Whatever wasn't stapled to the ground was overturned. It wasn't a major earthquake, just a small one, the kind that shook vases off their stands onto people's heads. The police took diligent notes and read them back to me. Later, they told me the blond girl had died on the floor. Her name was Shannon. Shannon had been very small.

The police asked me if I knew where the strange man had gone, but I told them I did not.

Do you know him? they asked.

No. I did not know him.

Ma'am, they said. When you're feeling better, we have some questions. Just routine. Are you feeling all right? Ma'am?

* * *

I found him in the corner of the trauma bay, cradling his body with his head pressed deeply into his jeans. I was shaking; he was breathing. When he looked up at me I was almost sick from the amount of blood on his forehead. I thought he was going to die, and it should have been me. This poor son of a bitch took a bullet for me.

Jesus, I said. Steady now. I can perform first aid.

I approached him with gauze. He had blue eyes, really awful clear blue eyes with a brown ring around them—I'd seen eyes like that before—and I brought the white to his forehead and wiped the skin. Just like wiping shit off the sidewalk. There was no wound, no entrance, no pain. He did not move, even when I dropped the gauze and backed away. This was worse than the man and the gun. I did not expect this.

They said the bullet hit you, I said.

He was gone a moment later when the attending physician found me huddled in the corner, as far away from the gauze as I could be.

* * *

I passed my boards with high scores, and after my pharmacy rotations I took a job in the ER. A layperson, or a nurse, would have normally been hired to take insurance and health history from walk-ins. Lizzy helped HR get past my over-qualifications: I know the effects of the medications the patients are popping and how they react to one another, I can better decide what is serious and what can wait, I can perform mouth-to-mouth.

During rotations, I sat behind glass and doled out meds to anyone who had a handwritten permission slip from their doctors, or gave generic Sudafed to kids who wanted to try to make meth in the trunk of their cars. After it exploded, and it always exploded, Lizzy would tell me about the way they looked with half their faces gone, and I tried to remember if they were the blue or brown shifty-eyes of the little shits who tried to sound stuffed up when they asked politely for little red pills.

Those evenings when I went to her apartment and sat at her cramped dinette, Lizzy would say it's inevitable that people hurt themselves. Don't feel bad. Hey, did you hear the one about the women with the IUD?

I hadn't heard the one about the woman with the IUD.

An ambulance whirred by, screaming, and we both listened.

She gets an IUD, Lizzy said. Doctor fiddles it up between her legs, pats her on the ass, and tells her to have a good day. Some months later she comes into the emergency room real dignified and dazed. She has a brown paper bag and she dumps it on the desk. It's a bloody fetus with the IUD stuck in its head. Dumpty-dumpty.

Oh yeah? I said.

She asks for a refund, of course.

Isn't that horrible? I said.

* * *

Lizzy and I went to med school together. She studied surgery; I stuck my nose in pharmaceutical textbooks. We took classes on medical ethics together. It was an easy friendship, someone to complain to about the job and who wasn't grossed out when one of us had to say she dug around in someone's grandmother that day. There was no danger of competing for residencies. We made a game where we would tell one another the worst stories we heard or saw while practicing, some of them so bad we said if it happened to us, or if it happened again, we would drop out and take up guitar like the other med kids who tried to pay their bills sitting on the corners strumming rhythm. Yet when it happened too many times that the ugliness became rote expectation, we told the stories and pretended to be surprised. Sometimes we told them with our mouths on one another's, and sometimes with our hands, but those tellings, those movements, were not permanent. Just an ache that needed to be expressed with bodies, and a familiar body was best.

What did the man look like, Lizzy asked me, after I told her about the shooting. The bulletproof guy.

Blue eyes, I said. Really blue.

Shit. I was stuck on a kidney transplant. Waste of a good organ. Woman's got an ongoing marriage of her lips on a bottle.

I thought she was at the bottom of the list.

She's got the money for a brand spanking new one, never touched a drop in its life. Your guy is in the papers, Lizzy said. They're calling him the Miracle-Man. You're not the only one. You heard about that fire on Fourth? The Catholic school? He saved three kids and their plaid jumpers, all of it. The kids were half burned, but he was perfectly fine. Not a scratch on him.

Jesus.

Sounds like he's going to get around to all of us, she said.

* * *

Within a week, the man was like an earthquake, touching everywhere you could see. They printed photos of what people thought he looked like—a mess of cheekbones and floppy hair—and discussed him on the evening news. They ran side-by-side headlines in the paper: *Unknown Miracle-Man Saves The Day* right next to *Unstable Grounds: Will Our City Crash?* Some of the smaller rags called him the antichrist, a fake messiah, and they claimed he was a sign the city was going to hell. The rapture, they said. Repent. They made up glossy brochures with warning signs of the devil and handed them out on corners. They left their palms out, spread, if you accidentally took one.

People were carrying signs for him, marching in rows down the streets, hanging their signs in their apartment windows, having them printed on T-shirts. There were all sorts of messages for him in English and Chinese and Russian. *Go away,* they said. *Save us,* they said. *Please help. We need you.* And others, *Miracle-Baby, marry me?*

He's like a pill, I thought. After swallowing, it's scientific magic, and suddenly or slowly everything fixes itself and you don't even need to know how it works. The only ritual is in doctor's scripts and cash exchange.

When I was a young girl, I thought illness was when the strands of the body that vibrated together became frayed, like strings in old sweaters. Pills broke apart, dissolved, and they would attach to those strings and unfray them, retwist them, heal them, make them new. But that's not entirely true. Pills retighten our muscles and our veins, making them unnaturally strong, keeping us together long enough to grow old and cultivate cancer. And you can't fight cancer unless you are willing to kill off some part of yourself. There is no miracle; there is only holding on.

And once we crack open, we are all infestation. Cranial fluids, spinal fluids, blood, and pus. One of the first things they showed us in school was the slow decomposition of a body. Within minutes of dying the cells break down and pollute with carbon dioxide. It starts in the stomach and spreads. In a week those gases reach the face. The skin discolors and begins to slide off the bones. The gases in us rise and release; we expand. We look like we're floating, a kind of rotting magic. That's why we have to get the dead in the ground or in the freezers or the fire as fast as possible before we witness this decomposition. When I first saw a body bloat twice its size, I vomited. I had to watch the eyeballs and intestines liquefy, then the muscular organs melt. The skin splits and falls off from our bones like finely cooked pork. The muscles turn into waxy soap. The blood pools on whatever side the body lies on, stomach or back. Like a rash. In that way, we are not so different from the rust on the buildings that house us.

Our bodies are only temporary; they are supposed to be temporary. But this man was not temporary.

* * *

I paid too much for my apartment, a shitty one-room fourteen stories high with a bed, a chair, a desk, and a fridge that was shorter than my chest. Everything in it was green, from the bedspread to the pale walls to the one picture I halfheartedly put up of a clock, frozen at five-eighteen.

It had a balcony allowing for a lonely freedom, somewhere to smoke so I didn't have to walk down the stairs and inhale with the rest of the people in my building. I liked inhaling and watching the filter spot with brown and black, the reminder of what I was taking in. At least I was taking something in.

I didn't smoke during the day. One too many people made just loud enough comments about how horrible it was to be a health-care professional and know how badly I'm fucking myself up. Or the short, fat ladies who walked by and coughed, that strained cough when their throats were clear, because they were too polite to say anything. Or the old men with polos and Bluetooth, saying what a shame it was, such a young thing like me doing this, and their mothers died from lung cancer.

At night I went out on my balcony every twenty minutes.

He was out there. That man. I didn't know for how long. The sun had not yet set, and I could see it fading on the mush-yellow threads of his hair. He hunched against the stone. His feet were bare.

I had a long knife for butchering beef off the bone, sharp enough to cut through fish scales and skin. I've never used it; I hate cutting into flesh. I held it in front of me and knelt in my kitchen. I watched him all night. He had a strong back, and I could see the outline of bones indenting his shirt.

He shuddered only once, a great heave that lifted his whole body into tension. I trembled the knife and closed my eyes. He was gone when I opened them.

* * *

Every night he was out there, whimpering when the sirens blazed past. Sometimes I only saw him for a few minutes before I blinked and he was gone, other times he was there all night, rocking, his hands around his head.

It was loud at night. I could hear the dim buzz of the lights, the automated bell of the convenience mart across the street banging when the doors open. The people laughing, sighing, talking down below. And the steady, impertinent jerk of the building, when everyone shut up for a second to wait and worry if something bigger was coming.

* * *

I had trouble sleeping at my apartment with him out there, so I asked Lizzy if I could spend the night with her. I didn't tell her about the man. I didn't think she would believe me, or worse, she'd want to come over and look. She didn't mind, said she liked the company. It's miserable to live with someone else sometimes, but even more miserable to live alone.

At night, I watched her undress down to her panties—striped blue boy boxers with ripped lace along the edges—and took pictures of her with her camera. She posed with her ass stretched out and her hair or her hands covering her breasts. Her hair was done in pigtails, long enough to almost touch the elastic blue band around her hips. She looked straight at the camera and smiled or pouted in turn. Sometimes, she asked me to only photograph her from the neck down.

After each click she bounced over and examined the photo and either pushed delete or handed it back to me. I took twenty pictures of her, and when we were done I helped her curl plastic wrap around her lower torso all the way down to her thighs. I waited outside the bathroom while she showered.

Once, when we were sharing horrible stories we had heard over drafts of thick beer—the girl with the twenty-pound colon, the guy who stuck the needle up his ass to see if he would get high quicker—Lizzy told me about the night she had been at a bar with a man she didn't like. She entertained him on boring nights because he was generous with food and drink, because he had been a lieutenant or a sergeant in the military, and because he always had fresh-cut hair and a firm chin. He continued to buy her drinks but stopped himself after two, and when he drove her home he drove to his home first and asked her to come upstairs. It was next to the train tracks. She remembered the trains very clearly. Perhaps he was threatening, maybe sexy, but Lizzy went up and slurred and had her body banged into the fridge. She banged against it so hard it fell over and, laughing, they stood it upright before collapsing on the bed like rag dolls. He was rough, and she had bruises and a urinary tract infection that felt like hot steel when the last train cut through her head and woke her up. She dressed and asked him if he came, and he said no. She felt around inside her, around the burn, and felt satisfied with his answer. She refused a ride and sagged home.

After, instead of sex, she posted pictures of her body onto hard-to-find websites. Men, maybe women, she said it was hard to tell from their usernames, would send her electronic money, and she would mail the panties, carefully folded into Ziplocks. The people who bought them, I imagine, spread the bag's lips apart real slow, like they were spreading her legs, and lifted her panties to their faces and inhaled, or maybe they put them on their tongues and rolled them about, like caviar, or wine.

She had started with shoes, but the money was in panties.

She was currently working on a special order for a man who believed she was nineteen and working her way through cosmetology school. For a thousand dollars she was wearing a single pair for two weeks and was not to take them off for anything; showering, her period, even to piss. She drew the line at shitting herself and said she cheated on the pissing part. She was going to pee on it the day she sent it. To cover the smell she doused her outer clothes with perfume.

It's not that I don't like sex with men, she said as I helped to remove the wet plastic paper. I do, I really do. It's just that I haven't been able to get it up, you know? This is safer. It's cleaner. Just me dirtying myself.

I helped her replace the wet plastic paper with dry, wrapping it around her torso. We clambered onto her bed because she only had a couch piled with papers and books and the clothes she hadn't bothered to carry to the Laundromat for weeks. She kept buying more clothes instead of taking them in.

She wore two pairs of baggy pants and a sports bra. I wore a long-sleeved shirt. It was hot in her apartment. I could hear the air conditioner thrumming, but it was half-hearted, weak against the heat.

You can take off your shirt, you know, she said.

I shook my head. I had not taken my shirt off in front of anyone for a long time, not even Lizzy. I could barely stand to look at myself without one on. She took off her bra.

Did I tell you the one about the girl with the birth control? she asked.

Maybe. Probably. Did it end poorly?

Always does.

Lizzy rolled onto her back and put her hand under her head. I could see the outline of her lips and the curve of her nipples in the low light. The blinds gently bounced against her open window. I rolled onto my stomach.

I guess her doctor didn't tell her how to use the pills, so she goes into the pharmacy, after about a week, trying to get her prescription refilled. Are you sure you haven't heard this one?

Sounds familiar. Tell it anyway.

The pharmacist looks through her file and tells her she shouldn't be in so soon for a refill, but the girl says she's out.

I reached my hand over to Lizzy's stomach, that smooth expanse, the small curl of her belly from hamburgers and beer on weekend nights. I watched her face.

She'd been taking them all right, used them all up. She put one up her vagina every time she had sex with her boyfriend.

Christ, I said. I spread my fingers over her belly.

That tickles. No, don't move; it's all right. I don't mind. So, the girl, yeah, she's got a terrible yeast infection. And on top of it, surprise, she's pregnant.

The small print is too small.

No kidding.

Lizzy put her hand on my back. I could give you a massage if you want, she asked. But this is nice, too. Your turn. Tell me one.

I haven't got one. Haven't been to work since the shooting.

Remember one.

I thought about that girl with her blue eyes. In our stories, we never really gave details, not about what the hump-dumps looked like, unless it was necessary.

There was this girl who came in during my rotations, I said. Near the end.

When you were working down on Lawrence?

Yeah, the small shop. She was getting her cocktail. Covered by insurance, thankfully. She was only sixteen.

How did she contract?

No idea. She had a baby, too.

I felt Lizzy's hand stroke the side of my breast. I stilled.

Was she breastfeeding? Lizzy asked.

I think so. Yeah. Two cocktails.

I rolled onto my hip and shoulder.

You haven't told me this one, Lizzy said.

No.

I touched her sweatpants with one hand and put my other near her mouth. She was smiling.

Go on, she said. Go on.

I felt the line of a scar on her belly, a line of reformed skin that never looks as pretty or feels like the original. Scars are too smooth to be like normal skin. They feel used, and so much better, like a small rebirth, a reformation, a testament to having experienced pain and triumphed.

Lizzy curved her hand on my hips. I closed my eyes and felt underneath the stretchy waistband on her lounge pants. The Saran Wrap was like her scar, so damn smooth. It wrinkled, quiet, but I heard it over the sound of the air conditioner, that weird unnatural smooth sound. I saw her hand moving under my shirt and went still. I removed my hand and rolled away.

Hey, she said. Hey.

I got up and put on my pants.

I can take it off, she said. He'll never know.

Is it a guy?

Probably.

I reached around for my bag.

Are you leaving?

I'm out of cigarettes, I said.

Are you coming back?

Outside, I lit up one of the emergency cigs I kept in a plastic box in one of the thousands of zippers in my bag. I smoked all of them on the way back to my apartment, a good twenty blocks. I checked the balcony when I got back in. The man wasn't there.

* * *

The earthquakes were getting worse. People with money or families out of state started a great migration to anywhere that would have them, but there were still many left behind. The hospital called and asked me to come in—we know you're not over what happened, they said, but we need you. The ER is full. A lot of them just need to be patched up. You can do first aid.

I let it go to voicemail. I considered showering to leave my apartment but eventually just left and picked up a carton of cigarettes and a case of diet soda. Lizzy called twice and didn't leave a message. I watched a lot of TV. Sitcoms. I couldn't stomach the news. I couldn't leave.

He was there when I came out of the bathroom after the sun went down. That bastard, I really wanted a cigarette. I considered sneaking downstairs, but being trapped on the elevator during an earthquake scared me. I hated stairs.

I picked up my boning knife and slowly opened the balcony door. He didn't move. I slipped the knife out in front of me and felt my way to the other side.

You just stay there, I said. You're trespassing. This is my balcony, so you don't get to make any movement. You can stay, but don't move.

I lit a cigarette and sat down. The muddy clouds were out, but even if they weren't, I wouldn't have been able to see the stars, not with all our light.

The man looked at me. Even in the dark his eyes were obnoxiously blue. I pointed the knife at him. Hey, I said, don't move.

He stared.

I butted my cigarette and lit another one.

I said, I guess it's polite to thank you for saving my life. You didn't have to, but thank you all the same.

He kept looking at me.

Do you want one? I asked. No, you don't. People like you don't smoke. One of the first people I saw cracked open was a smoker. Lungs were soot, all black. But that didn't make me want to stop. It makes sense. You know the health symbol, the snake and the rod? I always thought the snake was poisonous, and a rod, well, how the fuck are you supposed to heal people with that? Healing means hurting first.

He watched me. I watched him. Around us, I could hear the noise of the city, like the ignorant buzz of cicadas flying, and falling, when they hit a halogen light.

* * *

I grew used to his presence but thought of him as nothing more than a curious spider, the kind I used to have in my bedroom as a child. They would form their detailed webs in the corners, and I was too scared to kill them or touch them and put them outside and save them, so I let them stay until they died on their own because nothing fell into their nets. Eventually my father would come in and squish them in bunched up toilet paper, because it was kinder, he said, to kill them quickly then to let them starve.

I still took my knife with me. In case.

* * *

Lizzy kept calling and hanging up. The hospital stopped calling. On the news, they had experts and politicians recommending that people move or stay, depending on the station. They went out to get the voice of the people on the streets: What do you think of this man? Do you think he's really there to save us?

Man, said a teenager, the mic held up to his face. I don't know. He kind of, he kind of seems like he has to, you know? Else why else would he be here? What's he got to prove?

I changed the channel. This time, it was a woman with a pressed suit and pulled back hair. She was sitting next to an anchorwoman who looked the same, hair and suit, except the other was blond.

Hysteria, really. A red herring created by the media to keep us from talking about the real issues. Unemployment is the highest it's been in years, and with the earthquakes creating serious questions about our infrastructure, the politicos must have prayed for such a man to come along and confuse voters, to save them from the excuse to have to talk about what we elected them to discuss.

Have you seen this man? the blond asked.

Only pictures.

And what do you think of him?

He's handsome, certainly.

* * *

Lizzy left me a voicemail:

Why aren't you answering? Are you OK? I'm really worried about you. I have to talk to you, please; it's about that miracle guy. Do you believe in him? I didn't, I didn't, and I was wrong, I was so wrong.

She coughed for a second.

I jumped. I mean, jumped, she said. From the roof of my apartment building. I don't know what I was thinking. I lost this little girl on the table. She was seven, Jesus, just fucking seven years old. And I kept thinking how unfair it was, how useless I was. Why haven't you been returning my calls? I thought I was OK, you know? It wasn't serious.

And I, I just jumped. I didn't even think about it. I just wanted to get some air and then I thought about it and I didn't stop thinking about it. I jumped. I thought I was going to be some broken dumpty on the sidewalk, and they'd declare me dead and forget me in the morgue. But he caught me. He came out of nowhere. He can fly, Jesus, did you know he could fly? I really think he can save us. I really do.

She repeated my name over and over until it sounded strange and unfamiliar to me.

I dialed her number but ended the call before it connected.

* * *

He was out on my balcony. I lit up and offered him one, but he didn't respond. He huddled with his arms over his knees and his face smashed against his arms and watched.

Thank you, I said. You saved a friend of mine.

He moved his shoulders up, the barest of shrugs, but it was something, and for some reason it made me happy.

Take off your shirt, I told him on a whim.

He didn't move.

My hands were shaking, but I managed to get my shirt over my head. I didn't look at him but I knew he was staring at my breasts, and not in the way a man stares at a woman's breasts, because no one who had seen mine looks at them in that way. Your eyes remind me of this girl I once saw, I told him. She had horrible eyes. Yours are nice.

His arms dropped to his sides, and he moved closer to me. To get a better look.

Once, I told him, much the way Lizzy and I would tell one another stories. Once, there was a young girl who needed medicine because she was very ill. I imagine men like you don't get ill.

She asked me for her prescription. I didn't remember her, though I bet I'd filled it for her before. HIV-positive, stage three, so there were a lot of pills, a lot of checking in the computer to make sure that she was on time, that we weren't overdosing her, that we got everything right. You can't trust people to keep track of all of it on their own. She was supposed to pick up two prescriptions, and the computer said she always picked up two. One for her, and one for her baby.

I took a long drag.

I asked her, with a row of people waiting behind her, why she wasn't getting the medicine for her baby. I expected her to tell me that the baby had died, or was being cared for by someone else. I was prepared to be embarrassed for asking. She said, she looked at me in the eye and said that she stopped dosing her baby. She wanted to see what would happen to her if she stopped taking them.

I inhaled and exhaled.

I almost dropped my cigarette when he touched me, gently, like he was scared of me or scared I would move or yell. His fingers brushed the scar between my breasts, that long white and thick puckered line.

Accident, I said. I was on a bike and a car hit me. They had to crack open my chest.

Take off your shirt, I told him. Just take it off.

He lifted his hands up and kept them there, so I pulled the shirt over his head.

Don't move, I told him. I want to see something.

My father's boning knife was sharp enough to cut my finger when I ran my fingers along the edges, so I knew I wouldn't have to press deep. I put it to his chest, below his nipple, and ran it across. When there was no mark, I did it again, harder.

I bet you're jealous that you can't have a scar like mine.

I was angry at him, not because he touched me, not because he saved Lizzy and me and so many others and allowed all this madness to keep going on, but because he was distant, unable to tear or break, and all those miracles and acts of bravery he performed weren't really anything special.

I told him to put his shirt back on and he did.

He took the cigarette out of my mouth and put it in his own and breathed in. He coughed. It was such an unremarkable human sound, that weakness, that recognizable part of me that was ugly and yet, because he was nothing like me, I clung to it. I started crying in that way I didn't know you could cry, when all the water runs out of your eyes and you don't make a sound, but you can't stop either.

Thank you, I told him. Thank you.

I was grateful to him and sick for it.

* * *

When you cough your body goes through three phases; the inhalation, where you voluntarily take a breath against the scratches in your throat, knowing full well that what comes next will hurt, but there will be a sick pleasurable release as well. Then you force the air against your vocal cords, your glottis, and it spreads apart like thighs. When it opens, the air releases out your mouth, something violent, a quick noise, a harsh scratch. It is instant relief, for a few seconds, before the back of your throat tickles again.

You have to apologize afterwards, make amends for letting that small part of you out, or if you sneeze, invoke the divine. Lizzy was a great cougher, really loud booming, startling noises, and she never apologized.

In this way, we continue on—brutal hacking things.

* * *

I watched Lizzy on the news, saying what the man had done for her, how he had plucked her in the air. She was so happy, so ecstatic, but she lied and said she tripped over the edge. My stomach clenched. I'd never seen her so happy before.

Of course he'll save us, Lizzy said. She was in the midst of a mad kind of belief, and I never thought her as lovely as I did then.

We don't have to be afraid. We don't have to leave, not while he is here.

* * *

When the earthquake bounded across my room, I hid under my oak desk, like those kids did in the atomic age with their arms over their head. I was thrust side to side, up and down, and even though I had removed most of my objects to the floor and off the tables and the walls, everything fell over. Outside, I could hear short, quick screams, and the grumble and quake of pieces of the building breaking off. I tried to light a cigarette but I couldn't keep my hands from shaking, even after.

When it stopped I stayed where I was, even after the sirens awoke outside. I waited for the aftershock, a sign that the larger one had already happened, and it would soon be over.

The aftershock did not come. How long would we have to wait?

* * *

That night, I watched the figure of the man in the window of the high-rise across from and below mine. We were old stranger-chums; I had spent many mornings watching him over coffee as he struggled with his tie in his mirror or went to his own balcony and frenzied his hands at the pigeons. Though I've never seen him watching me, he must have seen me out on my balcony smoking and known me in that friendly, voiceless way, where you are so tuned to someone's habits you know them as well as your lover, except you do not know their name.

He stepped out onto his balcony and looked down. He was crying, great sobbing shoulder-hunching bursts, and put a gun to his head and pulled the trigger. The pop left his face a wound. His useless torso and limbs fell forward over the edge.

I did not look down at first. I knew what I would see: his body crushed under its own weight, and his pants soiled with the remnants of his colon, the last thing he would do. And then I did look, that long horrible glance, the fine sizzle of his blood in the heat, the body. People gathered around him until, slowly, methodically, they got on their knees and put their hands over the places where his skin had cracked and the wet oozed out. It was a fantasy kind of first aid, if you put enough pressure on the body it will right itself.

He had not inflicted a wound but exposed one.

* * *

Soon after they taped off the sidewalk and cleaned him off, the whispers started. That miracle man can't save us all, if any of us. He should have known that man was suicidal, sick. We're as alone as we always were.

The believers remained because they trusted in a man who sat on my balcony every evening and plopped nicotine in his mouth without inhaling. Others remained because they could not afford to leave.

The earthquakes were getting worse, stronger. They lasted almost a minute, now.

* * *

Lizzy, I think you need to get out of here.

Where the fuck have you been?

Listen to me. I can't explain it, but I think it's going to get worse. Have you been watching the news?

I have been calling you and calling you. Why didn't you answer?

They're not saying it, not outright, but this guy, whoever he is, he can't make the ground stop shaking. We're all going to get caught in this if we stay.

I almost called the police; I thought you were dead. For fuck's sake, why didn't you call?

Are you listening to me? You have to get out.

Get out? And go where? Look, this guy, you don't get it. He's already saved both of us once. He touched us, bestowed some magical shit on us or something. Why wouldn't it work again? Why bother to do it once if not again? What would be the point of that?

All the king's men, Lizzy. All the king's horses.

Well, she laughed, who the fuck tries to put eggs back together with hoofs?

I thought, only a fool would try with their hands.

Why did you leave me like that? she asked. Was it something I did? I kept going over it. I'm sorry. It didn't mean anything.

Don't say that, I thought. It all means something.

* * *

He was staring at my breasts again, so I took off my shirt and let him see. I handed him a lit cigarette.

I explained how when I inhaled it wasn't really supposed to go to my lungs, that was just an unfortunate byproduct. It had to get into my blood to feel good. In the lungs, there are millions of alveoli, little pink, hollow tissue, and they absorbed the smoke and drugs and spread it into my bloodstream. They were good little suckers.

Every time he tried to inhale he coughed.

A man died here, I said. My neighbor.

The man inhaled and did not cough.

You're getting good, I said. Now you'll start craving them.

He stood up and looked out onto the sky. There wasn't much to see up above, but across, we could see the lights, all the lights that people had strung up high and lit.

You should let us be, I told him. Go back to where you came from. We can handle ourselves.

* * *

I had a dream where Lizzy and I had purchased a special kind of house. It was made of endless rooms, the kind the psychotic architect cannot help but continue, for if it ends then so does he. There was a room with all sorts of twinkling lamps and soprano songs in the walls. In one room, there was a piano carved out of a tree, still stuck in the ground, but alive all the same. Blossoms fell onto it, and it was so beautiful, and I knew we could live there forever; we would never become bored, and never get lost, because we would always find something new.

We did not even have bodies, not really, we just floated along, floated into one another, a happiness in not being corporeal.

Then I looked at the vents where it was musky, and there, piled onto one another, were corpses, and I knew without seeing that the entire house was built with the dead in its walls. I called Lizzy over.

She screamed and screamed and screamed, but it felt right that we should build and live amongst our dead. I floated into the vents with the bodies. It was warm there, and honest.

I woke up and turned on the television.

Sunday mass. A man in black with bowed head and clasped hands:

We must have faith that he can save us, not because he can. We know he can. But we must have faith that we are worth saving. There is something in our history, in our foundation, in our lives, that is worth remaining for. If we leave now, we forfeit, we retreat, and all that we have made is dust.

* * *

I was on my balcony when the big one hit.

The dogs started barking first. Sometimes, with the quakes, they were so small that I heard some people could feel them in one room of a house but not in the others. This one was everywhere, and it was quick. I could see people in the building next to me slam against the walls, and their computers and TVs slide off their desks.

The building beside mine cracked, like a zipper opening up, and each side began to move away from one the other. Loose pieces fell off. People screamed along with the crashing stonework.

People were running out of the way, but not all of them would be fast enough, and the miracle man could not be there for all of them. Some could barely stand and were crawling on the ground, falling onto their sides. There was glass on the ground. If they lived, they would get infections and slow-die. My cigarette fell over the balcony, still lit, and it left a trail of weak fire in the air. There were many stomped cigarette butts on the ground. A little memoriam of my own.

The building was shaking hard, but I lifted myself up to the stone surface of the ridge. I could see St. Ruth's wobbling like Jell-O, and the dogs were barking mad.

And in the distance, the man, flying. Flying straight towards me.

I turned my back on him and jumped.

Falling felt like nothing, like being unconscious, like holding your breath really long until you're about to explode for release.

Still I saw him, rushing towards me—this man who could really do magic, just like Lizzy said he could. Lizzy, Lizzy, where are you now? Still here? Crouched under your desk, near your bed, your cellophane wrappings shaking so hard you piss right through them?

A falling object descends at an increased rate, meaning the farther you fall, the more impact your body has on the surface, the more it has potential to leave a mark. An object that is caught, however, must be caught delicately, without panic, else it will break.

I wanted so badly for the ground to catch me.

My arm twisted under me when we made contact. My bone, I know this feeling, was broken. His bones, under his skin that cannot have been skin, felt like steel. I screamed, but I was not louder than all the voices under me, rising up louder and louder around the sounds of our concrete toppling over, breaking upon itself.

He flew me up higher and higher until we were above the dust clouds and I could see St. Ruth's fall apart and all the descending buildings breaking away from her.

We went higher still. I felt sick.

Postpartum

ou must never begin a story with waking up, so let us start right before. She slumbers unaware of two small, dumb mouths pulling at her body, her children, those twins with fine hair and greedy eyes. One of each, a girl-child and a boy-child, naked and filthy, their genitals soaked with the grease of unattended months. They empty themselves as they crawl from her thighs to her breast, where they suck the ever-flowing milk. They smear brown and yellow. They chirp for more.

Asleep, she dreams: an old woman, a caretaker, removing cinnamon buns from an oven. It heats up the room, a smell of rich comfort. She reaches to taste the risen dough, but the woman gently forces her hand away; too hot little girl, not yet. The girl is unused to waiting, so the woman tells her to recite her daily lessons.

Keep my fingernails clean. Tie my hair away from my face. Press my thighs tightly together.

On your wedding night, what do you say?

Here I am, husband.

Yes child, and one day your prince will come. Sing with me now child, one day he'll find me, one day he'll save me, one day he'll take me away. Chapped skin on her fingers, the years compounded into the bony knuckles, a sheen of gray over her eyes, the old woman ices a bun with melting sugar. Eat it slowly, savor it, let it melt. There's a good girl.

She has been pricked twice; once, not her fault, her father was short on golden plates, and a fairy with thunderous eyes went hungry at the baptism. This fairy knew her own value and would eat on nothing less than malleable metals from some faraway war-torn place. She never forgot the slight, and later placed a thorn whittled with a sleep spell in a spindle, certain the girl would touch it when she was of age. The second time, not her fault, she was in her hundred-year bed, and a man with a crown on his head found her. Dazed and delighted, he bent over her still form and placed his lips on hers, found her warm enough. He undressed and climbed in.

* * *

The boy-child, with nothing to gnaw and his milk teeth aching in his mouth, begins to scour her body for something firm to connect with. By chance, he happens on the thorn in her finger and sucks with the same insistence of his father. It dislodges easily.

The dream begins to fade, and she fights to see it to its end. Give me your palm, the old woman says. I can tell you what your beloved will look like. Ah, see here? He will be handsome. He will be kind. He rides a great white steed, and he has got all his teeth. Close your eyes now; if you think hard enough, maybe you will see him, too.

Roused against the lethargy, she looks down at her body, the mold all around her from a wet bed, the dried blood between her thighs from a lonely birth, her breasts askew atop their dressing gown, the girl-child weeping against her arm and the smell of spice far away and fading. Desperate, she tries to hold onto that wrinkled old face, the taste of dough rolling under her tongue, but it dissolves as she opens her mouth. Unlocked, she attempts the eruption of a hundred-years-buried song in her breast, one she never learned, the long wail, but her throat is dry, parched, and all she manages is a whelping croak. Beside her, the girl-child, ecstatic to hear the sound of her mother, begins to wail.

Eden

Everyone called him a horse fucker, though not in his hearing. No one dared. Rolo had a mean face, like someone had pressed thumbtacks into his cheeks when he was a kid and the impressions remained like tired wounds. He never talked to anyone, and if you tried, they said his small eyes got even smaller.

Jim-Bob, Earwig, and I used to hang around the stables where Rolo worked on Mr. Scarsdale's farm. There was less to do there than anywhere else in town, but nobody bothered us, so if we wanted to smoke or drink the beer we hid under our jackets or look at my father's crusty nudie mags, we could do so in peace. Rolo kept to himself, minding the horses and shoveling shit out of the stables. For a long time I didn't think he knew we were there.

Of the three of us, Jim-Bob was always first to grab a beer, light a cigarette, or pull on his dick. He was named on account of his mother compromising between either of the two men who may have been his daddy. She never called him Jim-Bob. It was always one or the other, depending on which man she decided she liked better that day. Or maybe to make the other jealous. Jim-Bob had several theories. His mom smoked clove cigarettes every day and throughout every pregnancy, though Jim-Bob was the only one who'd made it out alive. She used to pull up her shirt and show her cesarean scar to anyone who cared to see. "Bikini cut," she'd say. "Right across. Like they were cutting down a tree."

We called Earwig after the little critters because he was kind of like an earwig, ugly and small but pretty harmless. When we showed him a picture of one he flailed his arms and shrieked, and so we kept showing it to him until it bored us to see him react.

The three of us were always looking for new things to get off to, especially around the Apple Fest when the weather was warm and dry and all the girls wore their clothes tight on their bodies and put extra wag in their hips until we were halfway mad. We couldn't get out of the town—the whole of our families broke bread and brow there—but we could get off on the town. It was Jim-Bob who'd found a picture of last year's Apple Queen in a two-piece, so we were spending the day masturbating over it.

"Where did you get it?" I asked.

"Dad's Bible. In Leviticus."

"Which dad?"

Jim-Bob shrugged.

Last year, the Apple Queen was a tall girl with long hair. Every girl in town wanted to be the Apple Queen, crowned at the Fest. It meant she was the prettiest seventeen-year-old around. This one had been especially attractive. She had blond hair. I liked blond hair. Hers was the palest I'd ever seen. Almost like fresh-fallen snow. I was in the middle of whacking away, thinking about her looking at me or maybe talking to me or something, so I didn't hear Jim-Bob or Earwig stop or back away. I didn't hear Rolo approach, or Jim-Bob do up his pants real quick.

"What're you doing?" Rolo said. "Hell you boys doing?" It was the first time I'd heard his voice. It sounded unused and that made it cruel. He was wearing a faded red cap, long unwashed strands of his hair falling around his face, the rest of it tucked behind his ears.

Jim-Bob and Earwig got up and started running without any care for me. Earwig was screeching, trailing his pants behind him like a flag. I didn't move. Up close Rolo looked like the boogeyman, except worse because he was real.

"What's this?" he said and picked up the picture of the Apple Queen from where Earwig had dropped it. It was crumpled, and there was a bit of Jim-Bob splashed on her belly. I didn't know what to say, or if I should say anything, so I sat there dumb quiet and watched him stare at the photo with a long and sad face.

"How old are you, boy?" he said.

"Thirteen. Almost fourteen."

"She ain't for you," he said.

I didn't know what that meant. I was going to ask him, but he turned around and said, "Aw, shit." One of the horses was hitting its ass against the fence, bucking its head and whinnying. It was a stallion. I could tell from here.

I noticed Rolo slipped the Apple Queen's picture into his dirty overall pocket before he ran off. For a while I watched him coax the horse. Even though he was probably a crazy fuck, I had to give Rolo credit. He stayed calm, even when the thing jumped and kicked its strong legs. A horse that size could take your head off. When he calmed it down they just stood still, both of them, staring at one another like they were both batshit or something. It was weird. That night I dreamed about horses running away from me until I couldn't see them anymore.

* * *

I didn't see Earwig or Jim-Bob again for a week after that, but I knew I'd see them at the Apple Fest. Everyone went to the Apple Fest except Rolo, and his lack of attendance was always spoken about in the beer tent, loudly or softly, because who else but a horse fucker wouldn't want to come and see an Apple Queen get crowned? Whenever he was the punchline, they all slapped one another on the back and laughed. Rolo was the easy joke. It united them. Even the women thought it was funny to laugh about Rolo. Often they wouldn't have anything funny to share with the men, but they could all laugh about that poor old horse fucker guy. I felt sick when they said those kinds of things.

I walked around with my dad until he abandoned me at the beer tent to be with his friends and tell his favorite Rolo story, though I don't think they'd ever met. Dad was always quick to point out how Rolo stole his job and everyone knew it because my father was the best farm worker there was and Scarsdale had the best farm and that meant the best money and weren't there enough people in the town to hire? Looking for outside help, my dad always said, was the luxury of the asshole rich. All the men would agree with him because they'd wanted that job, too, but they wouldn't have fucked a horse to get it like Rolo must have.

I found Jim-Bob and Earwig standing around the beer tent waiting to see if one of the fathers would get drunk enough and feel sorry for sober boys and pass them a cold one or two. I thought they were avoiding me because they were embarrassed for abandoning me with Rolo, but that wasn't the case.

"Did you bring it?" Jim-Bob asked me, flicking his lighter. He had a shiner around his eye. I didn't ask about it, because I could recognize that kind of damage when I saw it. Earwig only had his mother and three sisters, so he kept staring at it, but even he knew better than to say anything. Those kinds of things you maintained quietly, else you were a pussy.

"Bring what?" I asked.

He lowered his voice. "You know, idiot. The picture. From the Bible."

"Oh." I said. "No. He took it. Rolo."

"Shit."

I was giving Jim-Bob a "sorry-bout-that" cigarette when we saw her. Last year's Apple Queen. She looked better than in the picture, even with more clothes on. I couldn't remember her name, but I never could remember any of the names of the Apple Queens. You could always tell an ex-Apple Queen, even long after they became our mothers and grandmothers. There was something about the way they walked, like they were better than us, which I guess was true because they were better than us. Sometimes you'd see them walking around on a non-Fest day with their rhinestone crowns on their head, the sun hitting it and shining so bright it pierced your eyes to look at them straight on. Still, we all wanted them, better than us or not—still wanted to see what they felt and tasted like.

She was swinging a bright red leather bag on her arm. It looked heavy. She stopped in front of us. I couldn't see her eyes. She wore big dark sunglasses. Earwig and I held up our chests and stared at her full on. Jim-Bob was a year older than us and had more experience with girls, so he looked like he gave two shits.

She said, "Can I bum one?"

Jim-Bob gave her his cigarette. He held the lighter up to her lips. I was impressed; his hand didn't tremble or anything.

"You boys come to watch the crowning?" she asked.

We nodded.

"I was so pretty last year."

We nodded.

"Having a good time?" she asked.

We nodded.

"You gonna cheer for the new Apple Queen?"

We shrugged. It was the right response. For the time it takes to smoke a cigarette real slow, last year's Apple Queen stood next to us against the tent and puffed. Some of the men would occasionally pat her on the head or her ass and say, Hey, Apple Queen, hey, and sometimes she'd say hey back and other times she stood still like it hadn't happened. We thought it was real cool, like we were being real slick and all that because she stayed with us. After, we were going to leave without saying anything, because that's what you do with a girl, even an older one; you leave them wanting more. But Earwig opened his damn mouth and told her we hung out by Rolo's barn and she should come by with us whenever she wanted. More smokes, he told her. And booze.

"I know the place," she said. She said she might stop by in that airy way older girls had, and once she was gone Jim-Bob and I really let Earwig have it. We punched him on either side, hard, but he didn't cry because none of us cried from something like that.

We all went to watch them crown the new Apple Queen. It was a good day for it. Sometimes it rained, but today it was stark and sunny. While all the women sat around and smoked and whispered in one another's ear, the men took all the fruit they'd pulled off the tree branches until they'd left them bare and laid them all down at the new Apple Queen's feet. Then they took the crown and blue sash from last year's queen and gave it to the bright-faced new one. She was plump in the face and brunette this time and she sat high on bushels of red and pink and green and rotting brown apples and raised her hands above us all, all very pretty like. We all loved her with our eyes, except last year's Apple Queen. She looked like murder. Red revenge. Sure, she smiled, and her teeth were all straight and white, but she had the same expression my dad did when he takes off his belt in the middle of the day.

After the festival died down and the men had to be carried away by their wives and daughters, Jim-Bob and Earwig said they were going to go to the diner and get free sodas from Earwig's mom, who worked as a line cook and would sometimes slip us burnt toast and undercooked eggs if we waited around long enough. She was a tired, happy woman and we all liked her. On the weekends she worked as a vet tech, which I think she liked better, said it was more fun, but there wasn't enough business to do it full time and there was no husband for her to only work when she wanted. She was always extra special nice to us boys, and if we were good she'd let us watch her cut the dead animals open or throw them into the fire.

I said I might join them at the diner later, said I was going to try to get the picture back, but really I just kept thinking about Rolo and that horse. He'd looked at that stallion like I saw Jim-Bob look at last year's Apple Queen. Maybe the rumors were true.

When I got there Rolo was shoveling out heaps of shit. He fumbled with the shovel when he saw me. I should have asked for the picture, but he just kept looking at me like he didn't know what I was, even though I suppose we looked mostly the same, except he was older and dirty. I asked if I could watch him take care of the horses. He stared at me for a long while, and I thought he would refuse, but he just turned around and kept shoveling. I took it as invitation enough.

He took care of the stables for Mr. Scarsdale, who was rich enough not to live around us. Scarsdale grew up in the house a few over from where I was born and lived, but he had a good sense for numbers and cheating, so he'd made it out of here. The girls all wanted to be the Apple Queen, and we boys all wanted to be like Mr. Scarsdale, who could afford to keep this land for breeding and competition but didn't have to live on the shit himself.

Rolo worked hard and was real kind to the horses, kinder than my dad was with me, anyway. He really took his time with them, especially when he bathed them. He'd take a hose and wet the ground near their hoofs, then splash their legs. He spent a lot of time on their legs, smoothing the muscles there with his bare hands. He said you had to check the vein on the inside of the leg and make sure it was cool before you hosed their body, else they'd colic. Then he'd move up the firm thighs and massage them, then onto their shoulders before moving to their necks, their long torsos, and the tail. He shampooed their manes and tails and scrubbed hard, whispering cooing things I couldn't make out all the while. Then he'd put on their anti-sweat sheets and call them good boy or good girl, like my mom used to do when I was young and coming out of the bath. After, he'd cut up carrots and feed them. When the sun wasn't too hot he worked them around the yard, which didn't seem much like work. They liked to run, their long, knobby legs prancing like they were on show, and their tails shining. Rolo must have brushed them all the time to keep their fur that straight and that nice.

I think he must have been lonely, because he told me all their names without me asking. There was Pinky, Haze, the tiny white mare was Butler, there was Charles Schulz, and the big brown stallion who'd been angry yesterday was Strut. Strut was Rolo's favorite. I could tell. He took his time with Strut, whispered all sorts of soothing things, called him "a sweet dumb beast" and fed him red apples.

"Hey," I said.

"Yeah?"

"That picture."

"Yeah?"

I shrugged. "You still got it?"

He kind of turned away from me and hid his hand in his pocket. "Yeah."

"Can I have it? It isn't mine. I gotta give it back."

He took his hand out of his pocket and handed me the picture, except it seemed cleaner now than when he'd taken it. Washed, if you can wash a photograph.

"Shouldn't do that," he said, looking at Strut. "What would she think if she knew?"

I didn't know. She was an Apple Queen. How would I know what kind of things went on in her head?

"She looks like a sweet thing," he said in the same tone he used when talking to Strut.

* * *

Even after I gave Jim-Bob the picture back and he decided we shouldn't spend so much time near the barns ("Fucking horse fucker," he said. "Shouldn't be allowed to be in town. Pervert. Probably watches us and gets off on it."), I still kept going back. Sometimes I didn't talk to Rolo and he didn't talk to me, but he'd always let me watch, and sometimes he let me shovel out the shit which I didn't care for really but it felt good to clean something for the horses. My favorite was when he let me touch Strut. Not much, and never for long. Just a quick stroke of his nose or a fast pound on the flank. The horse was wild and angry, but when he was younger, he'd won a couple of races, so they let him do what he wanted, so long as he would mount a mare when he was supposed to.

I had to keep making excuses why I couldn't hang out with Jim-Bob and Earwig. Jim-Bob said, Fuck, whatever, when I said I was sick or I had to stay home and help my mom with something, but Earwig would get all quiet and say he missed me and he hoped I got better soon. I called him a dope, and then he said bye and hung up, but I felt bad for him.

I never saw Rolo anywhere outside of the barn. He must have gone out for food and supplies and things that you need, but he wasn't ever in town. Didn't he want a cup of coffee with the other old guys? I always offered him a cigarette because that was something you did with friends—and it would force him to go into town and buy more if he took to them—but he always refused. Said it was bad for the horses. Said it was bad for me, too, but whatever.

He wasn't a talker, but I could usually get him to talk about the horses. If I asked about what people said about him he always told me to shut up, but if I asked nice things he would talk back. Once he started talking without me having to ask anything.

"See that?" Strut was running and whinnying. I thought it was because he was pissed or something, but Rolo said it was because he was happy.

"He's fenced in," I said.

Rolo grunted and grabbed the cigarette from my mouth. He broke it in half and threw it behind him. "Strut's easy," he said. "He don't need things like we do. Just simple stuff. All sorts of ugly things don't exist in his world. The only thing ugly to him is the fence, but see there? He runs around it like it ain't there, so it ain't."

And Strut did gallop around it like it wasn't there, like he wanted to take the turns he did and not because there was wire and wood in the way.

"Think like a horse does," Rolo said. "It might disconnect you for a bit."

I could tell he thought that was a good thing. I tried offering him a cigarette again, but he said no.

It was Earwig who called me and begged me to hang out with him, so I cut an afternoon with Rolo short and met him at the diner. His mom said she hadn't seen me around much and made me a strawberry milkshake. Earwig lowered his head, waited until his mom had her back turned, and whispered that Jim-Bob was fucking last year's Apple Queen. I think he told me so that he'd have someone to spend time with during their act. He seemed more lonely than usual. But he was a good kid. A little off but good all around. For him I spent the next afternoon with Rolo, went home for dinner because otherwise my mother would have sent my father out, pissed off from working nine hours, to drag me to the table, and planned to spend the evening with Earwig and Jim-Bob.

We three met up where we used to go whack off together, but Jim-Bob had brought the ex-Apple Queen. We couldn't tug on ourselves with an Apple Queen around, especially if she was Jim-Bob's. Seemed rude. She wore a red dress that ended before her knees and didn't wear shoes. It was dark, but she wore sunglasses anyway. Her toenails were painted pink. Her fingers were dirty.

She brought beer, much more than we could ever get raiding our parents' cabinets or hiding bottles in our coats at the drugstore, and we got really trashed. Earwig didn't know when to stop, so he vomited, drank more, vomited again, and passed out, but not before he cried out for his daddy, wherever that guy was. Last year's Apple Queen was older and wiser and knew what to do, so she rolled Earwig on his side and said this way he wouldn't choke on his vomit or smash his nose and suffocate in his sleep. Apple Queens are sweet like that.

I kept staring at Jim-Bob to see what changed when someone fucked an Apple Queen. We'd all imagined what it would be like, but besides his clenched jaw and looking off into the distance, it didn't seem like much was different. He didn't even pay attention to the Apple Queen, and I felt bad because maybe they had a fight or something—people who fuck often do—so I made sure she always had a full beer and a cigarette in either hand. That made Jim-Bob even more quiet. He tried putting his hand on her bare ankle but she hit him, hard.

She said, "Show me the horses," and she said it to me. "Jim-Bobby told me you hang around here a lot on your own." That made Jim-Bob wobble to his feet.

"What are you pissed about?" she asked him. She was laughing.

"Nothin," he said. "I'm going home. Tired."

"Oh, fuck you," she said. "You're just a shit."

Jim-Bob took two of the better beers and walked off, muttering to himself the whole time.

I wasn't feeling right, so when she asked me again I shook my head. "Can't. Not mine to show."

"You can," she said. "I want to feel that smooth thing under me. What's a queen without a steed, huh?" And I knew then that she hadn't drank nearly as much as the rest of us had. Or she could handle it better. She grabbed my hand and led me, like I was some magic bunny foot that would get her through whatever barrier she believed was there but she didn't really need me. I was disposable. I didn't mind. Her hand was soft and dirty and that was OK. It was simple and I liked it.

She opened the barn door and I guess Apple Queens have a strange sort of strength in them. They don't look it, but they got it. She pulled me in and she was laughing.

We saw Rolo there and we stopped moving. He was only wearing an old pair of jeans and stood in front of Strut's stable, holding the horse's muzzle in his hands right close to his face. He had his eyes closed and he was touching his lips against the horse's nose and he must have been whispering something because I could hear the vowels drawn but I couldn't make them out. It sounded something really painful kind of beautiful like. It hurt to watch. I wanted to leave, but the Apple Queen pulled me forward. Rolo turned and saw us and he looked scared.

"What're you doin' here?" Rolo said. He jerked back from Strut. The horse whinnied and threw his head back, almost hitting the side of the pen. "Get outta here."

I wanted to but the Apple Queen kept dragging me. "Oh, wow, all that shit they say about you is true," she said. "You really do fuck them." She made it sound like that was so cool.

"I said go!" He looked at me, his face all red, his eyes almost all white and wet. I pulled myself away from the Apple Queen and stumbled to the barn door, but I was so curious that I didn't leave. I stood in front of the doors and watched the Apple Queen take careful steps toward him on her toes, like a ballerina.

She picked up one of the apples Rolo kept around for the horses. A green one with spots, the real sour kind. She brought it to her nose and took a big whiff and smiled. She stared at Rolo and bit into the apple, the liquid dripping out the side of her lips. She took the piece from between her lips and offered it, opened palm, to Strut.

"Don't," said Rolo.

But she winked and the horse sniffed her palm, opened his muzzle and, with his huge, blunt teeth and sloppy lips, gulped the apple piece up. The Apple Queen took another bite of the apple and swallowed it. "Sweet," she said.

Rolo grunted and rubbed his chest like he wanted to cover up.

"Aw, don't be like that, Mister Roly-Poly," she said, sitting on the side of one of the troughs. "You'll scare the kid." She spread her long, pretty arms and said, "I always wondered that about you, whenever they talked about you. Old Rolo likes to fuck horses. They say I'm too old to be the Apple Queen anymore, but that's just age. So what's wrong with you? Why doesn't anyone like you? Is it because you can't get a woman to spread herself for you? Come here," she curled her fingers towards him. "I can like you, if you want. Don't you want to know what you're missing?"

She fisted the hem of her red dress in one hand and lifted it, willy-nilly, like she wanted to get it over with. Then she laid back and parted her thighs really fast, balancing herself on the two ends of the trough. She wasn't wearing any underwear. Around her thighs, near her pussy, she had tattoos of thorns. I felt worse than I did before. I wanted to touch those thorns and see if I'd prick myself.

"Well?" she said when Rolo didn't move. "Ain't you gonna?"

But Rolo just looked scared. Like she was scaring a big old man like him, even though she was shorter and must have underweighed him by about sixty pounds. Strut was grunting and hitting his body against the side of his pen. Rolo kept looking at the horse and then back at the ex-Apple Queen.

She looked up at him, her eyes kind of wet, and she said, "We don't really belong here anymore, you know. Don't you get it? Don't you see? Don't you want to? Come on, I don't bite."

He shook his head. He didn't say no. He said, "Gotta take care of Strut. Yer scaring him. Get out. Get out."

Strut didn't look freaked or anything, but I didn't like the way the air felt, so I ran out of the barn and went back to Earwig. I wanted to leave but I couldn't just abandon the stupid kid. I pushed him and pulled him, but he groaned and wouldn't budge.

She came towards me like something beautiful and terrible, and I wanted to run but I couldn't. She pointed to the cigarettes, and I pulled one out and lit it and gave it to her. She said, "You saw, didn't you? In the barn. All of it." She looked at me, cold, her face squashed. "You like what you saw?" she said, sounding like she was accusing me of doing something wrong.

What could I do? I nodded. Of course I'd liked it. Thorns and all.

"How much did you like it?" she said, her voice soft and scary.

"A lot," I said but I didn't mean it.

She put her hand on my shoulder and pulled me close.

"What about Jim-Bob?" I said, grabbing her wrist.

"You're here right now," she said, like that was the best thing about me, and maybe it was.

She was my first kiss. She was taller than me so she bent down kind of low and licked my cheek. I didn't know what I was supposed to do, so I stood there and let her take my shirt and belt off. Her hands were cold. I didn't know your hands could be cold when you did this. She kept touching her lips to my chest and forehead, like my mom would do when I was sick with fever as a kid. I tried kissing her on the lips, and she let me, but it was awkward and stiff so I stopped.

We lay down together and she guided me in. I should have known what to do, because Jim-Bob had told me what it was like—he heard his mom and either of his dads all the time—but what could I do? I thought the thorns would scratch me if I moved too much, so she did all the moving. It was over pretty fast, and when she was done she got up and left without saying good-bye or straightening her dress or wiping what was left of me off her leg. Her cigarette butt was next to my head.

I stayed with Earwig until he woke. He said he hurt all over and cried the whole way home. That's the kind of sad kid he was. He didn't ask me about what had happened or why I was the only one there and that was good because I didn't want to tell him. I tried to think about the Apple Queen and how it felt to be in her, but all I could imagine was Rolo and how he'd talked to Strut and how that just seemed nicer.

* * *

I tried to go back to the barn after that and, I don't know, apologize or something, but Rolo wouldn't talk to me anymore. He wouldn't even look at me, so I stopped going around there, even with Jim-Bob and Earwig to drink and smoke and look at pictures. We didn't see last year's

Apple Queen anymore after that, either. I asked Jim-Bob what had happened to her and he rolled his eyes and shrugged and said fuck her. Everything just got quiet and boring after that, but then Mr. Scarsdale returned to town because he'd heard one of his mares, Charles Schulz, had taken ill. Everyone was talking about it, not because anyone cared about the horse, really, but because Scarsdale rode into town in a white Lincoln Town Car, and it was as big as a boat. Our dads spent their time at the fancy bar—The Apple Turnover—wearing their Sunday suits when Scarsdale was in town. I think because if he showed up there he might give one or all of them a job, but he stayed on his farm with Rolo. They tried all they could, but Scarsdale lost interest because he had enough money to do so. He sent Charles Schulz to the vet and packed up his big car and left before they had the results. Earwig's mom was the one who looked after her, and she let Earwig and me watch her do the examinations. Jim-Bob didn't have the stomach for the smell of animals.

"It's good for you boys to see how things work," she said, watching the horse roll around in obvious pain. She put her head down and listened to its guts and said there was a lot of gas. She used something called a nasogastric tube, which she put in its nose and it went down all the way to its stomach. It was hard to watch her do that to Charles Schulz. She was a big thing, really sleek, and I could tell the tube made her miserable.

She said it had to be colic and depending on which kind it was she might have to operate. While we were waiting for the results, she started shining up her scalpels and the saws. But it wasn't so bad, just too much solid food and not enough water. She gave it a stomach tubing, which put water in its gut and helped loosen up the food. Then when it all came out the other end, she spread it on a piece of cellophane and let us look.

"Apples," she said. "Horse musta been mad for 'em. Too much of a good thing, you know?"

* * *

Last year's Apple Queen waited to announce her pregnancy right before the new harvest. She did it by wailing and crying and saying how ashamed she was and only was coming clean of the crime because she couldn't hide it anymore—her belly was too round for an Apple Queen now, even an ex one—and she was too goodly-godly to get rid of it. And when people asked where she got it she wailed louder and said it wasn't wanted; she'd said, No, no thank you, no, in her shrillest voice, but it was Rolo who'd done it. He didn't just fuck horses, she said, but pretty ex-Apple Queens too.

My mother had been the one to tell me, shaking her head and saying what an awful, awful thing it was and clucking her tongue and staring at the ground. That night I woke up sick and ran to the toilet and threw up my dinner. I crept down to the kitchen and called up Jim-Bob and got one of his dads—I couldn't tell them apart either—and said it was an emergency and please could I talk to him. Jim-Bob yawned into the phone and said, after I asked, that no he didn't fucking fuck last year's Apple Queen. She was a frigid bitch who didn't fucking put out and who'd said that? Earwig? That kid thinks fucking is when two people touch thighs.

I heaved into the kitchen sink but there wasn't nothing left to empty.

In the morning before my father woke up to go to work I watched my mother slip on her fancy Sunday coat and take up father's hunting shotgun. She looked at me and smiled soft and told me to grab my coat and come with. As we walked, more and more mothers and their yawning sons poured out of their houses. I saw Earwig gripping his mom's arm and sucking on his fingers. He waved at me but looked tired and lost. Jim-Bob was with his mom, helping to light her cigarette as she walked. All the women had shotguns and were experts at handling them. They were the ones, not their husbands, who marched out into the middle of the night and scared off the yowling coyotes that kept their kids up. Last year's Apple Queen marched in front of us on the arm of this year's Apple Queen, brunette comforting blond. I kept staring at her round belly.

I held my mom's hand and tried to pull her back but she kept pulling me forward. We stopped at Scarsdale's barn and it all seemed so unreal, like watching a movie on TV. Rolo was in the barn brushing Strut. He watched last year's Apple Queen point to him and hold her round belly, and he seemed to accept the injustice of it for what it was, but he took hold of Strut's reins and tried to lead the stallion out of the barn. Strut got spooked by all the people and he jumped up and kicked his front legs. The women then began to shout about how the horse was tainted and oh what a poor thing and how kind it would be to destroy it.

I watched them run Rolo like he'd run a horse around the yard, except they ran him straight out. I saw Earwig's mom running out with her hacksaw in one hand and a spatula in the other. She was arm in arm with Jim-Bob's mother (both of them, I remembered, had been Apple Queens), whose shirt rode up, and I could see the scar that was left on her to bring Jim-Bob into this town, and I realized that's what women did: they cut or were cut open. Last year's Apple Queen just stood back and watched. I tried to meet her eyes—I wanted her to look at me—but she wouldn't.

Earwig gripped my arm and Jim-Bob's mouth hung open as we stood dumb and watched the women tackle Rolo and hold him down. My mother fisted her hand in Rolo's hair and held him still. They stripped Rolo down to nothing but his socks. He wasn't fat or anything, but he had the kind of flabby flesh you get from a hard life packed onto his stomach and his thighs, his ass. They held him between them and made him watch as they spoke kindly to Strut and pulled him out of the barn, all the time Rolo was crying softly, and he didn't say anything even when they used hunting knives and their hands to tear into Strut's trembling neck. They tore him apart. They kept saying, this is what you did to that poor girl, see what you did to her? I'd heard rabbits scream before and that was something awful and foreign, but when a horse screams it sounds closer to the screams we make: simple and terrified, and I wanted to be able to make that noise and save that pretty horse, but my mom, who I felt love for even then, raised a red brick and shoved it down hard on Strut's face and called it kindness.

Then they turned on Rolo and threw rocks at him and fired their guns at him and missed and said they wouldn't miss again. He ran and they chased. For a nude, scared man he ran quick, and they split us up to see if we could find him, making jokes that the one who brought back his dick would win a prize.

* * *

Us boys ran away from our mothers and the women, and we were the ones who found Rolo huddled beneath a pine tree, holding his pale body tightly in his tan arms and legs. I could see his shriveled genitals shining with wet and I knew he had pissed himself. Rolo looked up at me and said my name, quietly, sadly, asking for peace, a kind gesture or word.

"You know him?" Jim-Bob said, and I didn't know if he was talking to me or Rolo because he had a hard time looking at either of us.

I picked up a rock, a real jagged one. Earwig started whimpering and saying, "Hey. Hey. What are you doing?" He was looking from me to Rolo with a sad long face. He was too dumb to understand, but I knew Rolo was lucky because he had a chance to break free from all those things he loved and escape this place.

I screamed at Rolo and called him a horse fucker and threw the rock at his shoulder.

"Jesus fuck," said Jim-Bob. "You hit him?" He looked at me with a strange sick kind of awe, like even though we had just seen our mothers ravage all around us it had never occurred to him that we could do it, too.

Earwig was crying like the stone had struck him, but it was Rolo who was bleeding. Rolo didn't make a noise and he didn't move, and I wondered if he had even realized what had happened. So I picked up another rock and raised it high in my fist. I aimed it at his balls but I missed and hit the soft, white part of his thighs. Rolo yelped like an animal then and got up on his shaky feet and stumbled, his pale ass and balls bouncing, his thin legs running him away to somewhere far better than here.

Food My Father Feeds Me, Love My Husband Shows Me

My father is a great man of meat. Inside the hot, wooden house where the geese are kept, he stretches their long necks into straight lines and gavages grass and corn into their bellies, and when their wings can barely lift their plump bodies into the air he guts them and sears their livers with pepper and salt. In the pasture he keeps four fat, black cattle that he names after my forefathers: Luc, Pierre, Maurice, and Yves. When their bellies skim the ground he makes tartars of their loins with shallots and piquillo peppers. Then he buys four more fat black cows and names them Luc, Pierre, Maurice, and Yves. When he loves me best over my sisters he makes my favorite, *pot-au-feu*, and he cooks the meat so tender that no matter how much I suck on the flesh I still taste the bone.

I am often my father's favorite. When all my sisters put their white and smooth hands to their chests and faint at the gore on his killing smock, I gently untie its knots and wash it with my bare hands until they stain red. Because of this, my father gives me the first and largest servings of leg and rib, and when he boils lamb's head I am always allowed to chew on their glossy, black eyes.

When men come for my hand my father keeps them at bay by giving them the hands of my sisters, and they go gaily into common houses that smell of lilacs and goldenrod. But when the man with the short beard comes at night for a bride my father is all out of other daughters, and so he weeps and curses that he had not been given sons instead, for he would care less to lose a son. But my father must give me away, because a daughter is only a dowry to be won, even if he loves her as much as my father does me, even if there is no one left to care for him now that we are all gone, and my mother long dead.

The man claims to be no different than my father, for he too had once been a butcher, a great one, prolific in his craft. When he threw sumptuous feasts he would slaughter, by hand, fields of goats, sheep, and cattle. His hands confirm what he says, for no man that has slaughtered can hide the stains, and my new husband's are streaked dark red.

On our way to his castle the peasants we pass on the road avert their eyes to their feet. The old women, their head and eyes covered with black scarves, tap their foreheads, chest and shoulders. They wrap their gnarled fingers around giant crucifixes that weigh down their thin necks. I ask my husband why he is no longer a butcher.

He says butchering is in his past. Then he points to the dark sky and says, Each time the sun swings around the world we are all allowed to begin again, and he says this with such sincerity that I begin to love him.

We are married in a small ceremony attended only by his sleepy servants. He goes over the lines and movements as if by rote. On my hand he places a simple, thick gold band. He takes me to a great banquet hall for the celebratory feast, and though there is no one but us, twenty tables are laden with exotic cheeses and all manner of fruits. There are fifty different types of breads and all kinds of whipped butter, honey, mustards, oils. He slices apples and pears with an expert wrist, and these he hand-feeds me. Though I eat for hours from his hand, nothing fills me up as father's sliced cattle could, or a spoonful of his stews, or even a morsel of liver from a fattened goose.

After we perform our duty to our bloodlines, I lie on top of him and run my hand across the coarse hairs on his chest, and they are blue in such little light. I ask if I might be allowed to go to the market and purchase some meats, only a little smackering, for I crave it so.

He denies my request and kisses me on my forehead.

So I raise my leg high on his stomach and ask that I may have my father wrap and send me a little bit of beef, so small that my husband will not even see it, and I can consume it in a far, unused part of the castle.

Little bride, he says, do you not love me?

Of course, I say. And I do.

A loving bride fills herself with her husband, and what her husband eats.

Then he rolls on top of me, and though I love him, I cannot help but stare at his red hands.

Through the first month of our marriage, I eat nothing but soft cheese and ripe fruit, and though I consume enough of these sweet and delectable bites to serve a village, the hunger for meat makes me weak, and my waist and breasts shrink each morning I look in the mirror. The nights are torture, for I dream of fattening myself on tenderloin and pâté, and sometimes I wake up with my mouth smothered in my husband's hands, drooling and licking at the stains there just for a little taste. But I force my pride around me, close my eyes and chew figs and olives until I am ill. Sometimes, if I plug my nose, Gouda can taste like beef.

I ask once more for meat to quell my need, but my husband softly refuses.

He says, when I was a butcher, these hands (he holds them up before me and speaks of them as if they were a separate part of himself) clawed into tender flesh, and that the flesh of a lamb or a calf was not so different than that of a woman, or a child.

Oh, I cry to him, surely a cow's hide is different than a good Christian's?

He kisses the top of my head and tells me he loves me.

Do you? I want to say to him. Your hand-fed papayas and sliced Gruyère have shrunken my breasts, and made my hips as sharp at knives. But instead I lower my eyes and think of my father, and how he admires sharp knives.

My husband says I am to stay ignorant of such things. And though he holds me in his arms—strong, good arms—I smell the faint tang of blood on his hands, and curl myself deep into his body so I can be closer to that memory of meat. I salivate.

Is it odd, or wrong, to love a man's hands more than the man?

My dear husband is nothing but kind and gentle with me, so when he tells me he must leave for a few months to visit his homeland across the Himalayas, I fall on my knees and beg him not to leave. But he says he must. It is his duty to visit his lordly bankers and the tombs of his ancestors, and I must remain and watch over his vast home as mistress.

These are the keys to my kingdom, he says and slips a large ring with hundreds of keys around my left wrist. It weighs my hand down to my thigh.

What bride can expect that her husband, no matter how much he dotes on her, no matter how much he loves her, will spend all his time at her carefully laid table, or her freshly laundered bed? So I kiss every hair on his chin and tell him I will spend my days admiring every bit of his home so that when he returns I will truly be mistress, and the home will be ours.

Then he tells me of a room that I have not known exists and would have never known existed, a small room, in the west wing of his grand estate, and that even though I have the means to explore, I must not do so out of love. He picks the key from the ring to show me. It is haggard and thin, like a knuckle bone.

What is in this room that your beloved wife must not see?

Only memory, he says. Keep your mind like veal, *ma chou.* There is enough to keep you amused in my home.

From the highest point of his castle, I watch him leave until he disappears over the curve of the earth, and I wonder, if each man begins again when the sun rises, what manner of man my husband will be when he returns.

Our home is vast, and with no door locked to me, save one, I delight in spreading my arms and twirling in the endless china rooms, the rooms lined with swords and other instruments of war, the guest rooms with spiders nesting on thousand-count sheets. It is easy, when there is so much to look at, to forget for a time how hungry I am.

The servants quietly leave trays of oatmeal and peeled grapes and small squares of chocolate, but they run through me like water. Nothing sticks.

Soon, I no longer think of my husband or his wishes, but only my desire for heavy food. I write to my father: Do you still tie the knot on your smock too tight? I remember your hands were so lumpy that they would pull just far, and only my nimble fingers could release the cords. My fingers are even more nimble now, Father, like those small bones you softened in your stews and I would suck all the marrow until they snapped in half. Such bone-thin bones.

And I write: Father, you always forgot to clean your hands after you slaughtered Luc or Pierre or Maurice or Yves. Your hands were always so red, bright red, the red of blood that has not settled nor died. That is why I used to untie your smock for you, so that the red would not settle onto your clothes and bleed through to your skin and stain your body. It would be terrible, Father, to be forever marked, even if it was the thing you are so good at.

I receive no answer from my Father, so I write: Father, you would be so proud of my husband, for he is a good match. You have never seen your daughter consume so much bread and brie, and so much sherbet. But there is nothing here that tastes like what you make, Father. It is not that I am unhappy, oh no, but simply that we cannot forget where we come from, can we? Perhaps, if you have a few seconds to spare and some paper and twine, you might send me a bit of Yves, for he was always my favorite.

I write one more letter. Father, I write, send me Yves. Slice his throat. Hang him from his spine and tear the chunks of meat away from him until all that is left is white bone. Prepare it with salt, or smoke it, or bury it in the ground to preserve it, but you must send Yves to me. When you do, make sure it comes in to the back of the castle, for it is not that my husband is unkind or rules over me, but only he has a sensitive nose, and his stomach would turn at the smell of the thing I love. If you must, send me Maurice. I am not finicky. And I love you. Do you not know that I only ask this because I miss you so?

Each day that I wait for Father to send me the cattle named for my forefathers, I wander my husband's house, for nothing else keeps my hands from shaking, and only the sound of my hurried steps covers the sound of my belly. Too soon there are no rooms save those in the west wing, and because my belly shouts and I dream of rivers of flesh and black, blinking eyeballs (so succulent, so rare), I wander west, though I had promised myself I would not.

I think I imagine it at first—that I so miss my father and the way he showed me how to love—that my nose hallucinates. Behind the one locked door, the one that only the knuckle key fits, I smell blood.

Once, when I was very young, I stayed in the woods with my grandmother while my father took a summer to carry my mother from his bed into the belly of the dark earth. When I ate through my grandmother's summer preserves of smoked fish and fatty pork she sent me back to my father's home. It had been so long that I had forgotten the way through the forest. On the air I smelled the thick, rich scent of freshly spilled blood, and the particular salt residue I later learned was the taste of my father's grief. I have only tasted it once more, when Father made me *pot-au-feu* for the last time, the night before I married my husband. I will never forget the smell that led me home.

The air outside the locked door tastes like a salt lick, and I know this is a room of memory.

How is it that a knuckle-bone key can be so heavy? Yet, even if were made of real bone, or gold, or cold iron, it could not weigh so much. It rests in my hand like inevitability, and that is the heaviest substance. I enter the room forbidden to me, and there in front of me is all I have wished and longed for.

How did I ever doubt my father's love? It is Yves, sweet Yves partly wrapped in white linen on a stone table, his lovely body stretched out, his red and black muscles exposed and so very hot. I wave my hand above the offering and it is almost as if the tendons are still pulsing, like when a snake is gutted and its skin ripped off in one smooth strip, its long muscle of a body will still pulsate and writhe electric. There are lilies in all states of bloom and decay around the body. So strange, I have never been fond of lilies, Father, yet they look so pretty here, like little gay tongues.

Tenderly, since now that the feast is before me my desperation recedes, I tear a little bit of the flesh from the thigh, and what a thick one it is. I will not cook my first bites; I will eat them as the freshest tartare, so that none of the juice disintegrates into the air around me.

It tastes sweet and tangy, such tenderized meat. Father, you do love me best. You do you do you do. I never doubted it.

What a strange game my husband played with me, to forbid me from the room where he kept my father's love.

And what an odd room, for it is circular and along the walls is smooth mirror. I watch myself, as a familiar voyeur, placing those delectable morsels on my tongue. They drop like stone in my belly, and fill me up after the endless days of hollow bread. The blood smears on my lips and cheeks and chin, but what does that matter? If it fills me, I would smear red all over my body for the fleeting fullness of it.

I imagine it is rain, yes, rain, that falls on my head and rolls down my face. But the mirror shows it is red, and it slices my face through middle like a thin knife. There, hanging above me, are women's bodies in white dresses, strung up like scarecrows, each in a strange macabre pose. Stretched out, their necks hanging on hooks, parts of their bodies missing where the sirloin or flank would be cut. Long, lovely hair, golden hay, and chocolate drips cover their faces. I see, on their fourth finger, the sister-ring to the one around my own. Twenty or more women bleed above me, and I see an empty hook at the end of the line with a trail of scarlet covering the curve of the blade, down the wall, and up to the flat stone table.

For a long time I stare at the red tattoo on my face and call you Yves, sister-wife, but you are only my family in fate.

As I wait for my husband to come home I feel the familiar pull in my belly. The small taste of you was not enough to fill me, Yves, so I reach and tear a long strip of you. You fall apart so easily, like sliced smoked salmon, and you taste as tender.

Father, if I had a mother, or seven tall brothers, I may never have known what delicacies are hidden away behind closed doors. Soon, my husband will return to me, and he will look for me in the kitchen, then in his bed, and he will find me on my knees before his altar. My arm will reach towards him, and he will see the red trailing from my mouth. Father, you do not have to worry about your little daughter, for my husband and I have been laid out raw before one another, and he will love these fresh stains on my body.

three times Red

In Bed

t he beast told her to take off the frock and knickers, those extra human skins. But leave the cloak, such color, like cherry pie or tart flesh or a wound. Toss each piece of cotton and silk into the hearth and let it erupt. Come under cover and let me smell you, girl, let me smell your cloak, let me smell you.

The girl slipped her hands across the coarse fur of the imposter's massive and inert form. She grazed her fingers across the shallow belly and felt a familiar row of teats, like the ones that sprouted on her mother's breasts after bathing, or in winter after the fire went out. Surely, thought the girl, monsters could not nurse, could not nurture. The beast raised its heavy torso and the girl slid underneath.

Her mother had warned her before she entered the forest: be wary, little love; all things change in that darkness. Boys photosynthesize and girls erupt from the pupa, all thin wings and tongues peppered with nectar, and you can't ever go back into a cocoon. The walls have been ripped apart and cannot be sewn together again.

The girl's tongue flicked out and tasted the strange milk, a mother's milk, sweet and a bit salty, like a good cry. The beast whined in the low, soft way, like the girls' mother did at night when the window shutters shook and the bedroom was cold. It was cold every night since her father had gone into the forest and had not returned.

Photosynthesize, her mother said, looking out the window on those nights, her eyes reaching. It means you become a part of something greater. You can't go back.

The girl closed her eyes and drank the quick stream of sweet wetness that erupted from the beast. As she pulled on it, all the other teats began to cry, soaking the girl in thick, nourishing tear, and the beast wept as well.

Where does a monster feel loss, the girl thought—in the cavities of its jaw, or in its breast?

As she drank from the beast she tasted memory in that milk, her own and not only her own: earlier that day when the sun was high and before Grannie's house, she came across a string of pups, little more than stains, caught between a woodsman's steel teeth. Their necks were nothing more than sinew, long wet yarn.

She released the teat from her lips and reached under her naked back and fingered her cloak, wondering what dye had given it such lovely color, and whether she too could be made into mere stains.

In Belly

I wish we were face to face, Grannie, in this fleshy compartment. Instead, the long nail of your pinky toe, the one you adamantly refused to clip, as if it contained all your magic, curls around and in the soft skin of my nostril. When I breathe I can smell and taste all the places you have walked. You are still wearing your nightclothes, Grannie, that tired old gray shirt with the frayed edges. The hem rubs against my breasts like it did when I was a little girl, and you pulled me, naked as I slept, to you in those hot summer nights when I woke, drenched in wet salt, from nightmares.

The she-beast gulped me down with only my skin adorning me. Do you know she made me shave off all my hair, pluck every ingrown strand with black tweezers (I had to dig so far that I bled, Grannie), so when she swallowed me I slid down her throat like a skinned anchovy?

If you would speak to me, I imagine you would say what a funny place this is, where the walls are so warm as to burn, and the water is acid on our tongues. That's how you were, making light of what smothered us. There is only one bit of softness in here, and that is—how you would hate it—your breast, slipped from your gray shirt, as wrinkled as your cheeks and as veined as the raised lines I used to trace on your feet as a child. And when I grew up you told me to stop, stand on my feet, not my knees, and sleep with heavy nightshirts, and a towel wrapped tightly between my legs, because all manner of wetness could pour out of me when I slept. How I loathed growing up in those summer nights around you, Grannie, when I feared all of me would seep out.

I trace the lines on your breast while the walls of the beast clench and release and clench, and I feel you sliding away from me, Grannie.

Don't leave me alone in here, Grannie.

And then I, too, am pulled towards that tight opening, shat out onto the cold ground, leaves and dirt sticking to my face. Strange, only now I realize that I am covered, completely, in the inner slime of the beast's body.

Grannie, you're melting into the earth. Your old skin is falling off, your bones are becoming water and seeping into the mud. Will I too go quietly into the earth, as if I had never walked on its surface?

Yet the beast is tender, and before the sting of the sour from her belly makes me disappear like my poor grannie, she puts her tongue to my lips and moves up and down, cleaning me off, cooing as best a beast can coo. And when she is done, she spits, once, and looks at me in a way I have never been looked at before, like I am something new and something wonderful.

In Book

No matter how many times a girl has her story told, she will never be fully told up.

In one telling, our girl is shat out with the rabbits and dirt and the ragged flesh of her grandmother in one constipated pile. The beast buries her without turning around, simply kicking mud onto her face and shoulders, and wanders off. That one makes us ache in the spot our milk teeth fell from, and were abandoned, scattered under pillow or on the ground.

In another, the woodsman gutted the she-beast for food and warmth while his fair-haired daughter peeked from behind an oak with her eyes slit, for daughters never get used to the necessary violence of their fathers. When he saw the naked, hairless girl curled up in the beast's cavernous belly, he thought he had killed a pregnant werewolf. He grasped the smooth girl to his chest and would have torn her apart as he had her mother, but his daughter watched him and she did not blink. Instead, he took the girl into his home and fed her all the things he had slaughtered, while his daughter stared at the wolf-girl, watching each hair grow back on her body like corn shooting out of the earth, and wondered, her hands grasping her thighs, when the wolf-girl would sprout thick fur over her face and the back of her hands and devour them in the night.

In our favorite, the one we dare not tell, the girl rips herself out from the belly of the mother-wolf with her teeth and nails. Weeping, she shoves her grannie back into the belly and stitches it up until there is no seam. She curls into the mother-wolf and promises never, never to leave, and as she does, the mother-wolf turns into her own mother, a human mother. Together, they chase all woodsmen from their woods, and howl in a language we think we might understand, if we heard it.

But this is the one that was written, and so this is the one we tell to the shaking pigtails of our daughters and the fluttering eyes of our sons: A girl goes into the forest and is tricked by a man wearing a beast's fur coat. Because of this she loses her family, loses her innocence, and is saved by a man with a bloody axe, which is another sort of innocence lost. Then we do not know what becomes of her, whether she was happy to be torn out from under the beast, or whether she wished the bloody axe cut through her neck instead. Our children will make up their own endings, whether the girl becomes a witch or opens a cupcake shop or builds a bridge the color of gold. But we hope, in one of their minds, our beast-girl will find her gutted mother wolf, and using her hair as a thread and a curved toenail as a needle, begin to sew.

Let Down your Long Hair
and then yourself

My auntie said I should never know sharp things, because I was a sharp thing. I was made to cut, she said, not be cut. That was why she never allowed my hair to be shorn and let it pile up in the curves of my round room, on and under my bed, in the flowerpots on the sill. She never allowed me to leave the tower, because everything in there was soft. Beanbags. Blankets. Teddy bears. I would have liked to cut my fingernails with scissors, but since I was not allowed I bit them and swallowed the stale morsels. I spent hours stretching my skin and my muscles so that I could bite my toenails and taste the memory of where I had walked around my room, stepped on my hair, and where I could lick my sole.

My auntie said my hair was a coiled golden anaconda, sleek and cruel. My eyes were vultures. My teeth were as sharp as a wolverine's, my lips as red as the blood around its muzzle. I thought these words were sweet nibbles, because all I had known were soft objects and the cool palm of my auntie's withered hand on my face when she soothed me to sleep. I imagined these animals swallowing small soft things: little rabbits with their sinew bleeding out their necks or a beak as broken as a saw, carving into a dead baby bear cub, its eyes glossy and glass and dead. Such thoughts excited me when there was only velvet and linen to touch.

I strained outside the only window in my room and, in the distance, I could hear the world eating itself, tearing itself apart. I shivered, and I desired.

And then the man stood beneath my window and taught me what sweet words really were.

He called up, Hey bunny lady, you're a rare bloom. A rare honeyed butterfly with sun-tipped wings. You are peach fuzz. If you were my baby blueberry pie, I'd spend hours licking whatever drips between your pretty pink toes. Throw down your yielding hair so that I may wrap it around my tongue and only speak kind words forevermore. Throw down your hair and then yourself, lovely songbird.

What a handsome man, I thought.

My auntie wept when she saw me gathering my hair for him.

You are like your mother, she hissed at me.

I did not know her, I said, but I kneeled at her feet and touched her hem. Tell me about her. Was she sharp, like I am?

My auntie laughed high and cold. She was hungry, you wicked child. And when you were in her she ate every green thing she could see, even your father's eyes, which were as green as grass. And as she ate her bones stretched out her skin until she tore herself up from the inside.

Auntie, I sighed. I cannot stay.

She slapped me, but not hard enough to leave a mark. She was weak, at her age. Stab me, she said, stab me, you vicious, biting thing. Don't leave me alone with your hollow memory.

But I had nothing sharp except my teeth, so I bit down at her wrists and tore the flesh there. She bled all over my face. It was a strange, unsoft thing, her blood, all spice and sorrow. I held her until she died, and then I buried her in my beanbags, my blankets, my teddy bears. I threw down my hair and let the man yank my head all the way up.

When he saw the blood at my lips he said, your lipstick is smudged, my sweet hummingbird. Let me lick you clean.

When he pulled away, he licked his lips and stared at me and said, my dear, you taste like a warmed sword. When he said this he frowned.

I had no dress for my wedding. They used the yards of silk and lace to make trim for my hair, and for days ladies strung pearls and tied bows and weaved white and yellow blooms into the strands. When they had finally finished, and my hair was so heavy that I had fifty women in cotton shifts holding sections of it to march into the cathedral, the royal seamstresses said there was nothing left to cover me. Their stores were empty and the fields were barren stems and leaves. So I stood bare in front of the priest and my husband and my husband's mother and the harlequin courtiers. I considered being embarrassed but no one looked at my body. The men touched my hair and took discreet turns yanking on it—and how I could feel their soft hands, the little pulls growing into urgent tugs when I was to say my vows—and the old women weeping into its thickness with such passion that patches were drenched with their joy.

I did not sleep with my husband that first night, nor the next, not for a week after that. The ladies in waiting worked tirelessly to untie the silk and lace and drooping flowers and unknot each pearl, which they dropped into baskets to be given to the townspeople as a sign of our eventual generosity when my husband took his throne. But I saw the baskets with pearls go in a different direction of the castle, not to the front gates, but to the coffers in the dungeon, so that they might waste there with the thieves and murderers.

When we stood in front of one another, naked, expected to come together and form a child, our bodies glistened with the oil the servants rubbed over us, so that in the candlelight we looked like melting wax statues. My hair piled up in every part of the room, and when my husband made to approach me I cried out, Don't move, don't move, I can feel your heaviness in my strands.

We lay in bed as careful as baby birds. When he reached for me I felt the tugging at my scalp, and so I carefully unwrapped the strands from his wrist. He went on top of me, and he said, Sweet humming-bird, sweet girl, lovely late cherry blossom. He tried to be gentle but with each bounce my hair pulled underneath me, and when he was finished and lay next to me I reached up to soothe my head, and when

I brought my hand to my face there was blood sliding off the oil on my fingers.

When my husband closed his eyes, I put my fingers in my mouth. Oh, auntie, I miss you.

My husband is a boy. He takes care to shave each patch of skin on his body, and sometimes he uses silver tweezers to gorge their roots. Then he lets the servants into the boudoir, and they slather him in pale paint, filling in the holes, so that there is not a speck of red on him. He mumbles for days that he itches. At the long dinner table I see him sneak his hand into his trousers and scratch deep and long there, and then he sighs and smiles a bit. This is an ugly act, even my auntie would have agreed with me on that, but in these ugly moments I think I love him, and I want him to hold me down and scratch the gold between my legs, where it curls and knots and smells like sulfur.

My prince has taken to brushing my hair into a shine devoid of curls or knots. Then he splits my hair into three and carefully, reverently, his eyes wet and his hands trembling beneath the intricacy of the act, twists the lengths under and over one another. He does this for hours, never tiring nor stopping to relieve himself or to take a cup of warm milk, his favorite taste upon awaking and before retiring to his silk bed. When he reaches the split end of my hair he yanks it (sometimes so hard that I cry out, but I try to guess when he is about to do this and bite my lips together, for he looks so sad when I make such ugly noises, and he is so ugly when he is sad). Then he twists the end of it into a large loop, each time getting larger and larger, and ties it off with ribbon.

Look, he tells me, throwing the hair around his shoulders, we can fit both our necks in this.

Are you playing executioner? The hangman?

Don't be silly, he says. It is a scarf. Look how tight I have made the braid. Not even air will get between the strands.

I think not even our bodies will break them apart if we fall the entire length of the castle. I smile at him, for it is a beautiful noose, and I am proud that my prince can make such beautiful things.

When my clothes grow tight around my belly, I curl up in the barren room with my husband—what need have we of decorations, or a bed, or a blanket to cover ourselves, when my hair is so thick we can sleep on it and have no need for down pillows—and I tell him of my auntie.

She was a witch, I told him. She wrapped her hands around the cord that connected me to my mother and pinched.

Was she an ugly woman?

I've never seen my mother. I suppose she looks like me.

Your auntie.

Oh yes, I said. She had a turnip for a nose, and her skin was as rough as leather. She had coins for eyes—copper; they glowed in the night. And under her skirts she kept spiders. I leaned close to him and whispered, She used to say she liked the way it felt when the eggs hatched on her legs, all those little babies scrambling on her skin.

What a horrible woman, he said.

No, I said. She was lovely. She had cool hands, so cold, and at night she sang songs of the cave people. That is where they discovered fire, dark inside the bowels of the earth, and when they saw it for the first time they all went blind.

What a horrible story. Come, my love. He put his hand on my belly. Tell me of sweet things, you sweet sweet cherry stem.

I told him of the thing that was not in my heart: each strand of my hair was made of gold pounded thin, sprinkled with magic dust, and all who viewed it would fall instantly in love.

No one shall look at you then, he said, yawning and throwing his arm over me. As it grew darker, my skin numbed to him, and I could not feel the weight of his royal arm.

My daughter came out of me in an agonized splash. Auntie, I wish you were here to pinch the cord between us, to take her away from me, for she cries and cries. I cannot hear the sound of my own cries over hers. When the women reached to cut the cord with golden knives I screamed them away and reached between myself and strangled the cord apart.

I'll see her after she is cleaned, my husband said. Wrap her in cloth, white, and continue to wrap her until it is only white cloth.

Did he mean our daughter, or did he mean me?

Is her nose crooked? He asked me.

Oh, no, I said, and wrapped my hand around the braid he was tying off at the end. It will straighten. All little girls are born twisted, but they become like poles.

When my daughter was a golden two and clung to my legs, my husband's father died, and his queen, the dower lady of the castle, quietly followed him. The minstrels were ordered to make ballads of the intensity of their love, the sort that caused a worm to be wrapped around the heart and, when the other is gone, the worm begins to devour.

The crown my husband wore was gold and studded with rubies. The metalsmiths and jewelers, under my husband's whispered orders, cut the very ends of my hair, all of them split four or eight times, and after they slaved over their magic they trapped those snippets in the rubies so that, when the light hit them a certain way, you could see me trapped in so much red.

He was a kind ruler for a time, as all new rulers must be kind at first. He wanted nothing from our subjects, not their land for their food, or their daughters for his bed, and not even their sons for his army. Instead, he gave them seeds for the ground and dresses for their daughters and shoes for their sons. He raised his arms high, like he was reaching for the sun, and released the pearls from the coffers, and spread them like rain across the bodies of our people. Produce, he told them. Produce such lovely things.

Our daughter burrowed her head in my leg to hide her slanted nose.

After so many years he said, let us play a game, my golden egg.

All of his subjects were brought before him, no matter their age or station, from the shepherds to the ladies in waiting, and they stood before him while he looked them over and made his judgment. The sun hit the golden crown on his head and the light shined through the ruby, so that when they stood before him there was a red light on their faces or their breasts. And my hair, trapped in that light, split their bodies in half.

With my braid on his lap he said, Now this one, my little tulip, look how his face is scarred. What has happened to you, dear boy?

A wolf, my lord, said the boy. His knees trembled when the red light hit his eye.

No woman will want you, isn't that so?

I don't know, my lord.

Be kind, I said. He is so young.

He turned to the woman next to the boy and said, You are very horrible to look at.

Sir? She bowed her head.

Yes, your hair is string. Your face is sweet potato mush. Very dreadful.

Oh, I told him, she only needs a good scrubbing. These things will right themselves.

As do noses, my teapot?

Later, as I cupped my daughter's ears and hid her under my hair, she asked me, Mother, what is a sharp thing?

It is coiled, I told her. It waits to strike.

At the end of my braid I felt the weight of that boy, the old woman, and so many others, hanging, stretching my neck back until I feared it would snap. And, in the shaking tremor, I felt my husband's fingers stroking its thickness, gentle, like a bee landing on a petal.

We lay still until the screaming stopped.

They buried that young boy and the old woman, and so many others, under the moat. My husband worried that their bodies might bloat and rise up and stain the blue water brown, but the builders and buriers, with their hands placed across their moles, their scars, told him that once you are buried you will stay down.

They are so lucky, my husband said. You were the last thing they felt. Such strength in these strands, such softness.

Our daughter fears you, I told him.

He was wrapping my hair in a bow—a noose with two sides, and a knot in the middle.

Oh, my buzzing bee, my purple rose, you yourself cannot stand to hear her weep.

She does not weep any more.

When will she straighten? When she bleeds? That cannot be too long, now.

He cinched his noose very tight, and I felt the old wounds open on my scalp. I reached up and brought the blood to my lips.

Dream of the West, he told me, don't do that. It bitters your taste.

I waited until my daughter bled before I struck, the day before my husband was to have a grand party, to dress her in white cotton and parade her in front of him like any common woman born of the mud. I kept my hair in the braid he so loved and unwound it through the castle. He spent hours following it, like the string that led the man out of the labyrinth. When I felt his tugs growing weaker I shook the braid to renew his journey, and when he reached our bedroom he huffed and puffed like the old wolf from the story my auntie told me.

Come to bed, I told him.

He fell onto my braid-bed, and soon he was asleep.

Gently, I raised the small flap of skin over his eye. What blue eyes you have, my husband, like moat water.

Gentler still I reached behind his eyes with my nails—filed sharp, just like you would have liked, Auntie—and plucked them out. They were so small and delicate, real soft things.

He screamed. And cried. I did not know you could cry without eyes.

When he asked, pitiful bleats of noise, I said, it was the father of the boy, the one with the scar across his face.

Hang him, said my husband. But that is too kind. Rip out his tongue first.

But my husband, I soothed, he has such a lovely tongue. It is like the turning of the leaves, colorful, and to silence it too soon would be a crime, would it not?

Something must be done, he said. Something must be done.

It will be, I said.

When he curled his broken head into my lap and grasped my thighs, I knew you would be proud of me, Auntie. You wouldn't have done it any differently.

My morning dove, my husband reached for me, what does this woman before me look like? Is she beautiful?

He waved his hand in the air. I grasped it, rubbed it against my cheek, and placed it on my hair. He sighed.

I looked over the woman before me. She scrunched her face into her hands.

My lord, I told him, she is twilight. She is the moon. A pale beauty, like the sweet petal cheek of a chrysanthemum.

My husband sighed again. How wonderful, he said. I held his hand down when he went to scratch at the bandage on his eye. And this man?

He is iron, my lord. A sculpture made into flesh. His eyes are sapphires, his hands are fluttering butterflies.

The old man before me wept, but quietly, so my husband would not hear.

The guards brought me the heart of a thick-pelted boar. I kneeled before my husband and presented it to him, delicately squeezing it so my nails would not puncture the slimy thing, so that he would think it still beats.

Is it his heart, he asked me, the man who stole my eyes?

His heart lies at your feet, my husband, see how it quivers now, away from its body? Soon it will no longer move at all, and your revenge will be complete.

My crooked-nosed daughter watched me present myself. She has eyes like coins, and whatever she sees, she counts and discards, only keeping the important lessons in her head. This is one, I know, she will remember.

I had my husband's eyes covered in iron, and a crown of spikes cast for my head. At the center I placed his eyes, always open, never blinking, on top of one another. It did not fit on my head at first, for my hair was too thick, so with my husband's tweezers I spent a year digging and yanking each strand at its root until I was as bald and smooth as his body. I had my hair braided and tied off and made it into a whip. When I wanted my husband to follow me, I shook it in front of him.

My daughter's nose did not straighten, and soon my skin became as cooked and creased as that indent on her face. I watched as my husband felt the skin of a young maid, not yet the age of bleeding, and sighed so happily when he ran his hands across her skin.

I had the leather makers kill the calves as soon as they dropped from their mothers. They made a suit of baby skin, and I slipped into it each morning before I sat beside my husband, and at night he would spend hours running his hands and his tongue across the bellies of beasts and tell me what a smooth stomach I had, like water. The skin was thick. I felt nothing.

Suburban Alchemy

When he discovered the *albedo* in the moths' eyes and not their little hearts he fell to his knees and wept. He had been so foolish. It was a beginner's mistake; everyone went looking for answers in the heart. Most metaphors locked the soul in that rubbery, rhythmic thing, though it was little more than blood and salt. The walls of his lab were covered in tiny hearts pinned up, opened wide, drained, each in various stages of rot.

He could hear his daughter stomping around upstairs by the door to the basement. She must have just gotten home from school. He turned back to his work.

The early alchemists were obsessed with hearts, too. The greatest fallacy of the craft was that alchemy sought only to turn lead into gold, though any amateur could spin straw into glittering metal, and straw was easier to acquire than lead. That lie kept greedy rulers reaching their stingy fingers into coffers, funding the craft. But there was truth in the lie: alchemy was transformation, to take the worthless and make it worthwhile. And, the Alchemist thought, bitterly placing the extra, tiny hearts into Ziploc bags, what was more worthless than death? At least he could still use the fresh hearts in aphrodisiacs, or tinctures for jaundice.

Daddy, his daughter whined from the door. Dad.

Solanum, he called up to his daughter. What do you think moths did before light bulbs were invented?

Uhm?

Compared to its body, a moth's eye is enormous and oddly structured, made up of tiny crystals that twist and bend, deflecting the light. His current subject struggled in the tweezers. He asked it for patience while he spread a piece of wax paper over his work table, making sure there was enough room so as not to tip over the mortar and pestle, the looking glass, the spindle.

Dad!

I think they flew into the sun, he finished, using another pair of tweezers to pluck the eye. It thrashed so hard it tore the fine and fuzzy film of its wings. After he removed its other eye and gently placed it on the paper, he crushed the moth in his palm. Then he took a sharp knife and lifted his right sleeve where he had ticked off how many moths he had used in bright red slashes. He held his breath and made a quick stroke.

When Solanum was young he had no trouble getting her to join him in his work—though he never made her hurt herself if that was what the magic required—and her participation always yielded better results. At eleven she refused to understand that alchemy was a bodily experience more than a science, one that required giving of oneself for an effective return. She said she was too old to be torturing animals, even if it was for a good cause. He didn't think she was too old. Was eleven too old?

I'm sorry, what was that, dear? he called up.

I said I'm going to kill myself!

Oh. He adjusted the fire under his beaker. Oh! Wait a minute! I'm coming up.

He apologized to the moths in the jars along his worktable and ran upstairs. Solanum held a knife and a piece of paper. The latter she thrust into his hands.

What is this?

My suicide note, she said, holding the knife at her wrist, nowhere near the pulse point. Read it.

He read half. Solanum, he said slowly, mindful of her mental state. This isn't very good.

What?

This part, about your life breaking into meaningless pieces? You spelled it like peace-on-earth peace. Tumultuous only has one L, though I am proud of you for trying new words. Oh, and here your logic is faulty.

He pointed to the second paragraph. See, you start off with the argument that you have nothing to live for because nobody likes or understands you, but then you go on to say you'll be missed by—

I hate you! she dropped the knife. I really, really hate you! She took a deep breath. I'm going to Beth's.

Oh, he said, the letter drooping in his hand. Are you going to be home for dinner? I can make lasagna?

She slammed the door.

* * *

There had always been a bit of the illogical in Solanum. He understood her need to push against his authority, and to have one's blood tempered by whimsy, even the dark kind. In an art that required sacrifice, things often needed to be done on feeling.

The Alchemist thought perhaps he had damned his daughter when he named her. He had thought it amusing, once, to name her after nightshade. A small joke, but then the girl had bloomed deadly, and his lovely wife Sarah had dried up like a sun-soaked prune when baby Solanum splashed out.

Sarah would have been the good parent. It was she who dreamed each night their daughter would resemble a swan. He thought it was because he always compared Sarah's neck to the delicate bird. And he had wanted Solanum to look like that, too, because looking at two visions of his wife would have been better than one. That's simple numbers. But now there was only one, and her neck was nothing like a swan. It resembled a hippopotamus. It wasn't a bad thing. They were powerful animals, but when he'd told Solanum that she'd started crying and refused to speak to him for days.

He pulled out a journal with her name along the edge in black capitals.

Hypothesis, he wrote. *Solanum is insane.*

Proof:

Dilated eyes, heavier than normal breathing. Obsession with screeching Britney woman getting worse. Refuses to eat dinner. Crackers and bread are missing in the morning. Displays perpetual signs of anger.

He underlined anger.

Possible reasons:

Insufficient vitamins and minerals? Imbalance of the four colors?

In alchemy, the four colors needed to be in harmony for the magic to work. All four were in all living things, but most had more of one than the others. The foundation of the body was the *putrefactio*, the black, that which is stagnant. All alchemy began with death. His current work, bringing Sarah back to him, started with her ashes.

What followed was the *albedo*, white, something to burn out all impurity. Those were the moth eyes, or specifically, the tiny crystals in their eyes that did not reflect, but instead bent light to a sharp focal point. He still needed to find the *citrinitas*, the golden light, and the *rubedo*, the red, which unified the limited and the unlimited.

He supposed he could use Sarah's ashes in a concoction to heal Solanum's attitude as well, but he was wary of using too much on anything other than resurrection. And anyway, with Sarah back in their lives, Solanum would be OK.

* * *

The Alchemist ground the moth eyes down into a fine dust with the mortar and pestle. It was a long process; breaking down the body into the micro always was. Sweat dripped from his forehead into the bowl, but that was acceptable. The best alchemists always put something of themselves into their work, always of their bodies.

He heard Solanum descend into the lab, but he didn't look up, lest he frighten her away. She took little notice of the loose moths flitting about, or the smell of their decaying innards propped up and pinned down. He turned on a heat lamp over a pile of recently dissected eyes to dry them out. Carefully, he poured the already pulverized eyes into flasks.

He fumbled with a beaker when she spoke. Solanum, he said, you know you shouldn't disturb me when I'm working.

She frowned. I have to talk to you.

I'd like to talk with you, he said, pointing to a diagram. It had been so long since he could discuss work with her, ever since she was seven and said it wasn't cool to pluck the feathers from dead baby birds anymore. She got that nonsense from her mother, who had also been exceptionally squeamish. He said, Did you know that the cube is the most unnatural shape?

Dad, she whined.

You'll never find it in nature. Anywhere. Perfection is unnatural, but so powerful if achieved. He glanced at her. Do you have any idea why?

She sighed. No.

Something to strive for, perhaps?

Solanum waved her hands above her head. Dad! Dad! I got my period.

He beamed. Really? How exciting! Did you save it? You know, the first menses can be used for a very powerful rejuvenation potion. Let me grab a clean test tube and we—

I didn't save it! She looked mortified. That's gross.

You should have told me earlier, he said.

She stared at him like he was a curious-looking beetle, something to examine under a magnifying glass and then crush under her foot when it got too close.

It's most effective, he continued, for you. The bleedee. It could save your life in a crisis.

He watched the muscles in her jaw clench. Fascinating. He'd have to remember to write that down in his notes when she wasn't around.

* * *

The Alchemist disapproved of Solanum's desire for white plastic and cloth to staunch the flow. He told her they interfered with the body as a well-oiled machine. The excess should flow out. Letting it set inside was akin to fermentation and rot. Solanum told him he was stupid and didn't understand anything.

Sarah had only rolled her eyes at him when he told her the same thing, but she quietly snuck out of the house once a month, and later he would find the reddened tampons, wrapped in tissue, shoved to the bottom of the wastebasket.

They drove in silence. His knuckles whited over the steering wheel. She kicked her legs back and forth in nervous, arrhythmic jerks and fiddled with the radio. He wanted to listen to the local station's special on Burmese soloists, but Solanum didn't like culture. She twiddled the knob until she found her beloved Britney woman, screeching the same phrases over and over, nonsensically, crooning like a confused songbird. He wondered what Solanum found so appealing, but whenever she tried to explain the music, something about men and women and them all loving one another, he never really saw the appeal. He knew Sarah would have told him to keep trying, so he asked, Who is this, again?

She glared at him. It's *Britney*, Dad. She's like, really good. She's got a whole bunch of singles.

Singles of what?

Music singles.

Oh.

She's really beautiful, too. Solanum added.

Her voice doesn't sound real, the Alchemist said. Do you think it's metallic? Maybe she has too much iron in her system, or she swallowed mercury.

Solanum waved her arms. You're missing the point, Dad. She's so cool. She dances and wears halter tops. And her husband is super hot. She got him because she's so thin. I'm so fat.

You're not fat, he said, though he supposed she was a bit chubby.

Yes I am. She grabbed the fleshy pouch on her stomach and pulled. Everyone has skin like that, he said. He rubbed at his own stomach.

Sarah had worried about getting fat when she was pregnant, and he had not understood then why it was such a concern. Your body is supposed to change, to mold into something new, he had told her.

Then you change, she had snapped.

Sarah had read fairy tales and fables throughout Solanum's gestation. It's funny, she said, how many children get eaten up in these. Swallowed whole. Betrayed. Lost. Even the animals can't keep their young happy. They get rid of the ugly ones. They turn them loose until they aren't ugly anymore. When they're pretty they get to come back home. And everyone loves them.

My dear, he told her, those are old stories. It's not like that. It probably wasn't like that when they were telling them.

I know, she said, and held her hand over her swelling stomach. I know.

The Alchemist told Solanum, Remember that story about the ducking who thought he was ugly, but—

Dad, she interrupted, I'm not a bird. If you tell me I'm a bird, I am going to throw myself out of this car.

He wondered when she was granted the gift of exaggeration and desperately wished he could make a tincture of veritas for her, but he was out of anteater ears.

Instead, he asked, Who says you're fat?

Everyone. People at school.

The Alchemist shrugged. Everyone says I'm crazy, but that doesn't make it true.

When he glanced at her she was staring at him with wide, sad eyes.

* * *

They stood in front of the feminine needs aisle, a first-time event for the Alchemist. He stared up at the fluorescent lights above him, pulled out a notebook, and jotted down a few thoughts. Look at how they glow, he said. Solanum shoved a box into his hands and asked what he thought.

It was a generic, cheap brand. He grimaced at the silhouette of a woman mid-dance, her body curving so harshly it seemed she might fall over. There were large green letters on the side, promising a safe and easy fit. Comfort, guaranteed. You won't even notice anything is there at all.

The Alchemist put it back on the shelf. Something else, he said. Although he wished Sarah was around for considerably more selfish reasons, he wished she was here to respect this ritual properly for Solanum. He had no idea what part of himself he should give up to appease her body, and its changes.

He shrugged when she asked his opinion again, and let her wander through the Tampax, Playtex, Kotex, Lil-Lets, O.B., and others. She eventually chose Playtex and Kotex, which made him suspicious that she chose them because they rhymed. Before they left he picked up several long fluorescent light tubes.

On the ride home Solanum examined the boxes like they were new toys. She even let him tap his fingers on the wheel to Gregorian chant on the way home. Success, he thought. Perhaps he could buy her tampons every day. Then again, maybe she was enchanted by rhyme. So he repeated in his head, Playtex. Kotex. Kotex. Playtex. And then, Tex Mex. He pulled into the drive through of a Taco Bell and purchased them both burritos and several tacos for Solanum, because she requested them. She ate them before they made it back to their driveway, her mood souring with each bite. By the time he shut off the engine, she was screaming at him for making her fat, and how dare he want her to be unpopular. He watched helplessly as she ran into her room and slammed the door. When Britney blasted from her room he took out his notebook and underlined *insane* four times.

* * *

Before Solanum there was glittering hope between them, like an umbilical cord. Sarah whistled to little Solanum because she did not know how to sing, and in bed, at night, she held the Alchemist's hands to her belly and told him he was inside of her, both of their parts layered, like a matryoshka doll.

He rubbed oils over her belly and back to ease the pain of her expanding body. He did not tell her there was his own semen in the mixture, and she thanked him when he lifted his hands from her. That helps, she said. It smells horrible. It feels good.

Sarah's body would not change fast enough for Solanum. She did not gain enough at first, and then she gained too much. When a certain number of months had passed, the water inside of her leaked out like a broken faucet, and her body would not dilate. Though the Alchemist wanted Sarah to give birth at home—so many things he could have done for her, so many tinctures and potions he could have made to ease the birth—she was old fashioned and wanted it to be done with men who had stethoscopes and women with soft voices and soft hands, and needles that went into her spine.

The umbilical cord came out first, and the Alchemist wanted to ask if that was him, falling out of her, but the doctors and nurses rushed him out of the room. Later, he learned they cut Solanum out.

I couldn't feel anything, Sarah said, holding onto him, before she had seen Solanum for the first time. I was awake and I could hear her screaming, but I didn't feel a thing.

She's a swan-child, just like you wanted, he lied.

She wouldn't look at him.

I could have helped you, he said. I could have made it easier. He rocked her back and forth.

You're pulling at the stitches, she said.

* * *

There were four messages on the phone before the Alchemist played them. He often could not hear the phone in the basement, and told Sarah, who begged him to have a line installed there, that the noise made him jump.

I handle a lot of delicate creatures, he told her. They easily rip apart.

He had been working on an order of organic backache soothing balm for the young wife obsessed with breast augmentation down the block. She said his medicine was the best, and her husband was willing to pay a ludicrous amount for what essentially were a few plants and beetles he found in the garden, ground up and liquefied.

He pressed the button on the machine and looked in the fridge for some leftover lasagna to heat up for lunch.

This is Marion Thomson calling from Emerson Elementary. Solanum had an accident at school, and we think it is best that you come and pick her up for the rest of the afternoon. She's all right, nothing serious, but we think it is best if you came and took her home for the day. She's very upset. You can call us back at—

The rest of the messages were similar.

We're sorry to continue calling you, but there aren't any other contact numbers listed in Solanum's files, and Beth Pingree's parents are at work.

Please, she's very upset.

He arrived at the school twenty minutes later. Solanum was in the nurse's office, a coat he did not recognize draped over her lap. She looked up at him. Her eyes were red.

The nurse gently patted his shoulder. It's all right. Just a little embarrassing. Happens to a lot of girls. You can give the coat back to me on Friday, Solanum.

Solanum tied the coat around her waist and slipped her hand into the Alchemist's.

The nurse stopped him before he went out the door. I'll be over in a week to pay for the pills, she said. It's amazing how fast they work. My doctor said he's never seen a liver so healthy.

In the car, Solanum said, I didn't use the tampons. Like you said.

Oh, Solanum, he said. Your mother used them. I'm so sorry. Don't listen to me. I'm an old fool.

Solanum put her head into her hands.

That night, he gave her a large bowl of orange sherbet and sat with her. They watched cartoons.

The coyote is a lot like you, Dad. See? He's always making things. Solanum smiled up at him. She had big teeth, too big for her face, just like his own.

* * *

He didn't see Solanum for days after the school incident. She came home crying on Friday and said the others called her things. Red Rover. Red Tide. Cottonless Pony. She blamed him, and he had not known what to say, so he averted his eyes as she yelled at him and cringed when she slammed doors. He made sure she had dinner on the table, even if she didn't eat it. She was to and from school on time even if she opted to get a ride with her friend, Beth, and refused to let him pick her up. As the parent he knew he should be the one reaching out to her, except he didn't know what to say. The only time he saw her was when she was in front of the television in the family room. She was always in shorts and a bra, a sweatband across her head and one on each wrist, jumping up and down along with some fit women on the screen. Whenever he asked what she was doing, she glared at him and said, It's none of your business, followed by, If you must know, I'm going to look like her. She showed him a picture of a blond woman with a yellow anaconda draped across her arms, wearing brightly colored rags, her flat stomach sweaty.

He stayed in the basement.

He spread a thin coating of Sarah's ashes on his worktable, like dust. Using tweezers he dropped some of the moth eyes onto it. They sparked and fired up into glowing balls, like St. Elmo's fire. He watched, amazed, as they burned red and yellow. They fizzled into little black balls that broke apart when he touched them.

But what to do to maintain the burn? He had never tried to do anything this complex before; it hardly compared to making truth serums and headache relief concoctions. Resurrection was a myth, practically biblical, but that did not mean it was not possible. He made notes in the notebook with Sarah's name along the spine. He knew he was close; he could feel it trembling in his veins.

Sometimes he wished he could let Sarah be, yet every moment around Solanum was slow torture. She looked so much like Sarah. They had the same gold hair, the same eyes and fingernails. It was getting to where he almost could not remember what differentiated Sarah from Solanum. Was the smile he loved each morning the memory of the mother, or the slack-jawed joy of the daughter as she listened to that Britney woman? He did not recall how Sarah brushed her hair, but he remembered brushing baby Solanum's pale strands into gleaming gold.

He wondered if it was wrong to sometimes desire a dead wife over a daughter, and what from himself he would have to give to have them both at the same time.

* * *

Sarah was fanatical in the home after Solanum was born. He almost did not recognize her. She barely let Solanum out of her sight, and her whistling became shrieking jerks that would wake him in the night. He'd follow her to Solanum's room and see Sarah hovering over the crib, her lips shaped like a steel O.

I can make something for you, he told her, to help you sleep.

I just want to watch her, she said.

While Sarah bared her breast to Solanum and hiccupped at every drop spilled from her, the Alchemist descended into the basement and plucked the wings from gnats and the eyes from newts. He boiled them and spit into the mixture and used egg whites to make it taste better and sugar cane to sweeten it. He gave it to Sarah and she drank all of it in one gulp.

Sarah slept, and he held Solanum for the first time. The baby was not a bird at all, but a scrunched up prune.

When Sarah awoke she screamed. Where is my little swan? Where is she?

The Alchemist stood between Sarah and the crib. She's sleeping. She'll be OK.

I need to watch over her.

Let me help.

I don't want your help. I can do it.

For days, she stayed in the bathroom with Solanum. He put food at the door and could hear her sniffing every bite. She wouldn't drink anything he gave her, but he could hear her slurping at the faucet through the door.

The Alchemist thought, she will get over this. She will be normal again when all things pass.

* * *

Solanum came home from school when he was giving their neighbor, Mr. Johnson, a tonic that would extend his sessions of intercourse with Mrs. Johnson. The Alchemist had been providing this service and similar others to the neighborhood for quite some time, and when she was alive Sarah used the now dusty computer in the bedroom to sell his tonics and toxins to people all over the world. At present he only provided them to people who wrote to him or sent him checks. There were several packages piled up by the door that he had to remember to bring to the post office, but he kept forgetting.

Solanum glared at Mr. Johnson so obnoxiously the man started to tremble and almost dropped the tonic. The Alchemist crushed Mr. Johnson's payment in his fist. Same time next week? he said to Mr. Johnson, who nodded and tipped his hat to an unresponsive Solanum.

When Mr. Johnson was gone, Solanum turned on the Alchemist. Why can't you be a lawyer like Beth's dad? she whined.

The Alchemist felt tense. Beth's dad was the most boring man he'd ever had to interact with at rare school events that Solanum accidentally told him about. The man cared nothing for the property of bat entrails, for pity's sake.

What's so great about being a lawyer? he asked. I can turn trash into food. I can make light where there is shadow. I can bring the dead back to life! What lawyer does that?

She didn't answer, but he heard the hiccup that preceded her sobs. Solanum, he said, then sighed and rubbed his face. He asked if she would like to assist him. She always used to, when she was younger, when she thought playing with bugs and rodent innards was fun.

She rubbed her eyes with her palms. They call us freaks, Dad.

Who does?

Everyone. And they're right. They say you never leave the house and you're a mad scientist who's going to blow up the school.

The Alchemist frowned. That is patently untrue. I'm more than a scientist, I'm a—

You're a freak and you made me one, too!

She ran up to her room and slammed the door. Then the Britney came. He caught some of the lyrics, something about being stronger than the day before. He scoffed and went into the bathroom to wash his face with cold water.

Some swan child, he thought. For all her intelligence, for all her compassion, Sarah never would have thought that by wishing their daughter resembled a swan she inadvertently wished her mean. Hadn't Sarah known how aggressive and ornery those things were, for all their elegance, for all their grace?

He caught sight of the *rubido* bunched up in toilet paper in the middle of the wastebasket. Solanum's *rubido*. He bent down and examined it. Smelled it. Exactly as he feared, it had fermented in her body. Yet, there was power in blood, even clotted, old and black. And there was so much power in this sample. It was half his, half Sarah's. All sorts of love wrapped up in used cotton. He closed his eyes and fisted it, feeling inexplicably guilty, like he was doing something terribly wrong, but he wasn't sure what.

There is nothing wrong with love, he told himself. Nothing wrong with love.

He carried it into the basement and put it in a pot of boiling water. There was still some of Solanum stained on his hand, and since blood rituals always needed a greater sacrifice than a simple cut, he thrust his hand into the boil and held it there until he almost passed out. He cried out to Sarah until the only red on his hand was his own bubbling tissue.

Just the *citrine*, the gold, remained elusive, he thought, hunched over, cradling his hand. Then she would come home.

* * *

Solanum frowned when she saw his bandaged hand.

You'll have to help me, he told her. That only made her frown more, but she stiffly nodded.

He felt uncomfortable asking her to touch Sarah's ashes, or the congealed blood, so he had her hold crystallized moth eyes up to a magnifying glass.

Find twenty of them shaped like triangles, he said. Ninety degrees if possible.

He handed her a thin piece of metal with a tipped edge so fine it was barely visible. He said, Carefully, and I mean carefully, make a hole through the middle after you find them. Gentle. Don't crack them.

She worked quietly for a time, and he thought it nice. They were bonding.

She said, If you're going to be a freak anyway, why don't you make something that'll make me pretty?

He looked at her, really looked at her. There was nothing overtly wrong with her skin or hair or eyes, so how could she not be pretty? But Solanum knew more about these things than he did, he supposed.

Alchemy doesn't work that way, he said. You have to give something to get something. You know how it is.

She put the moth eyes down. It isn't fair, she said. How come I don't look like Mom?

He thought about how, when she announced her pregnancy, Sarah held his hand, even though his was covered in cat intestine, and told him not all magic was worth the sacrifice. It had just been some stray they'd tracked for hours and Sarah had cried over it even though she wasn't a cat person. Her face was blank as she watched him hang it up, its head still together, its body little more than bloody strings, but her eyes had been soaking wet.

He'd wanted to cut off his toe that night, said it was worth a perfect delivery of a perfect baby, but she had said she wanted to leave it to chance. She should have let him cut off his toe.

He thought about Sarah's soft hands, and he said, She was beautiful.

Oh. And I'm not? Solanum asked.

I didn't say that.

You just did! And I don't look like her so I'm ugly.

Your logic is very flawed sometimes. The Alchemist made to rub his eye with his damaged and swore when it ached.

So now I'm flawed and I'm fat and ugly. She slammed her hands on the table, mixing the moth eyes she had drilled amongst the others. Several fell to the floor. She said, All you care about are your stupid gross bugs!

Solanum, you stop it right now! I didn't say anything like that. He swore again when he involuntarily clenched his hands. He said, Maybe your mother was more beautiful than you, but only because she listened when other people spoke and didn't put words in their mouth or listen to shit music all the damn time. If I could instantly transform you into someone good I'd give anything for it, believe me!

He regretted it, but he stood rigid and still when she started to cry, when she pushed herself off the stool with deliberate slowness and walked upstairs. The door closed gently behind her.

He wanted to go after her, but helplessness weighed him down. He didn't know what incantation he could say to heal her, to bring them to convalescence, or what part of himself he could disconnect from his body to fix all worldly wounds.

* * *

Postpartum, the stethoscope men said at the checkup. You need to take it easy.

It feels overwhelming, Sarah said. All the time.

It'll pass, they told her. Take these.

They gave Sarah pills that made her pass out and stare at walls. But she moved out of the bathroom. When he went in there for the first time in weeks the bathtub drain was clogged with excrement.

She needs to stay on them, the doctors said. Don't miss a dose.

He hated the way the pills made her listless and content, a dense sort of happiness. He couldn't see himself anymore in her, not in her eyes, not layered in her. She showed him the cesarean scar and said, You can touch it if you want to. This is where they took Solanum out of me, and she sounded so pleased. She'll spread wings. She'll block out everything with her wings, you'll see.

Baby Solanum had no wings, just fat little arms and a scrunched face. The pills, he thought, were not helping; they were making her delusional.

Where are you, he thought. And where am I in you? He could not see himself at the edges of her scar, or at her eyes, or when she craned her long neck and opened her mouth; there was none of him peeking out inside of her, just her tonsils, and darkness.

It was easy to replace some of the pills with his own: little amounts of ambergris and rat urine, his eyelashes, and the small white flakes of skin that fell off of Solanum. He replaced just the ones on top first because she would not let the bottle out of her sight for very long, and he had to wait until she was turned to the faucet to fill a glass of water.

They were supposed to work, of course they were supposed to work, but she had said, They're not working, not like they used to.

Give it time, he said. Just give it time.

She took them all, his and the others he had not touched yet, in one big gulp that drowned the whole house.

* * *

It took him weeks with his bad hand to find and drill enough moth eyes. Solanum had barely spoken to him and he had not known what to say to her, so beyond putting food on the table and cleaning half-eaten plates he wouldn't have known she lived there. She didn't slam the doors anymore and if she listened to the Britney woman it must have been very quietly. He took careful notes in his notebook, writing and underlining *depressed* each day that went by without a sound from her.

He told himself that once Sarah was back everything would be OK. He told himself this every hour.

At least the alchemy was going well. The *citrinitas* eluded him but he was hopeful. He kept the blood in seal-tight tubes in the refrigerator and hollowed out the fluorescent tubes he had purchased when he had gotten Solanum's tampons. The *citrinitas* would hold everything together and maintain the burn, he was sure.

He didn't know Solanum was home until she started screaming. He had become so used to silence he feared the worst. He took the stairs two at a time and saw her, whole and sound, and thanked any god that was listening that she was OK.

What? he asked, testy and grateful.

Look, look! She was pointing at the television. A breaking news special was on. OUT OF CONTROL? it said. They were showing footage of a nonchalant bald woman wearing a tank top and sweat pants at a tattoo parlor, blandly looking through art.

The commentators said, From her sloppy appearance to her new 'do, has Britney lost her mind?

The Alchemist scratched his head. Is this the same Britney person you like? he asked. Maybe it wasn't. This woman looked tangible, a far cry from the plasticine woman on the posters in Solanum's room.

She nodded and said, She looks just like me, now. Solanum went up to the TV and traced her hand around the bald woman's protruding belly.

Well, maybe, the Alchemist conceded. Except the hair.

Solanum smiled up at him and ran upstairs, giggling as she went. It had been so long since he had heard that noise that he followed her up the steps, mesmerized. In his bathroom, she picked up his electric razor and blew loose chin hairs away from the blades.

I can do alchemy, too, she said.

She put the razor to the top of her head and clicked it on. Sarah had bought him that razor. He watched, fascinated and lost, as she dragged it through her head in uneven, slow strokes. Long chunks of her hair fell on the floor. It was golden and fine, like silk.

Carefully, he took the razor from her hand and, even though she protested at first, he cut away the chunks she missed. She smiled up at him, really smiled, her teeth as white as Sarah's.

Thank you, she said, shaking her head. I feel so light! She gave him a hug and held on for a long while.

It was less nerve-wracking to pocket her hair than her blood. She watched him curiously as he explained that she had the *citrinitas* in her all this time. Golden light wrapped up in thin, long strands. She smiled at that. He tentatively asked her if she wanted to help him and she nodded and followed him down into the basement.

As she watched, he took the ash and the blood and mixed it with purified water into a thick paste. He rubbed it on the surface of the moth eyes until they were entirely covered. With a needle thinner than a pin, he asked Solanum to thread it with her hair and put the moth eyes on the strands, tying them off at equidistant points, until they were strung up like a necklace. He attached this string to the inside of a fluorescent light tube and covered the ends.

They watched as the moth eyes started to flicker and smoke, and the strand of Solanum's hair shined. He explained that the eyes, the blood (he did not say whose), and hair would create an athanor, a self-feeding furnace to maintain temperature, but when the ash burned up it would explode and send out a signal, a beacon into the place Sarah remained, and she would see it and miss them and come back.

But what do you have to give up? she asked, bobbing her bald head up and down.

Remember what I said about moths flying into the sun?

She shrugged.

It mesmerized them, Solanum. They couldn't look away. And as they flew up their eyes melted, but that was OK because they could still feel the wonderful heat.

Daddy, she said. Daddy.

He could feel her mood plummeting, so with a whoop, he picked Solanum up under her arms and lifted her, ignoring the sting in his bad hand.

I'm too heavy! she cried, but she laughed when he put her on his shoulders and wrapped her hands around his head.

The light from the tube was brighter than fluorescent, and it was hot, like a kiln. He told Solanum to close her eyes and just feel, but he kept his own eyes intent on the light. To make the magic work, the Alchemist had to keep his mind solely on his goal: he imagined Sarah's ashes coming together, clumping and reforming. He remembered how cool her skin was when he lay next to her in bed and she would listen to his ramblings of color and creation and, when he talked too much that he could not turn himself off, she laid her hands over his eyes until all was blackness, and he could rest.

He imagined the ashes lightening from dark gray to a soft white, the color of her skin, and he remembered how Sarah dipped her head over her protruding stomach, her golden hair covering her face, her hand reaching out to take his and place it on her belly. Listen, she said. And feel. This is my magic. Swan magic, beautiful magic.

When he imagined the shell of her skin stretched out and pale, he thought of the blood running inside, filling up her veins, swirling mad in her heart until it moved on its own. He imagined a river of blood flowing within her, sealed up this time so that nothing inside of her could flow out, and she could contain him in her, and she could contain her little baby girl again.

And poor Solanum, who had a graceless neck and a mean, pinched face, but when she was happy could out-smile the mother she had only seen pictures of. Solanum, who —when she was five— dug up hundreds of pill bugs in the yard and kept them in glass jars because she insisted that they could be used in a happiness tonic to make the Alchemist smile (and, indeed, when she shook the bottle and whooped at the sound they made, they could). And when she was just born and opened her eyes and looked at him, those gray-blue muddled eyes, he had seen both Sarah and his daughter at once in her red face, looking at him with the same curious stare, and then Solanum had shut those eyes, balled her fists and wailed.

Daddy! Solanum cried, You're going to drop me!

He grabbed onto her legs and held on tight. Solanum wrapped her arms around his head and burrowed herself into him. He struggled to imagine his wife while Solanum squirmed on his shoulders. And they were so much alike, how could he differentiate them in his head? So he thought of their golden hair, the strands that had wrapped around his hands when he slept, or the hair he braided into two thick strands each morning for years, the hair that always smelled like warm cooking, and the golden strands he helped shear and used to string up moths' eyes.

Oh, Daddy, Solanum said, it's so beautiful. Can you see it? The light?

Solanum! Don't look!

It's so bright.

It was brighter than a Ferris wheel, brighter than a spotlight, or the sun. It blazed into him, a strange magic, and he fell to his knees. He tried so hard not to blink, but the tears falling to his cheeks burned him, and his eyes were drying out like the moth eyes had under the heat lamp. He wailed, and with one last cry to Solanum to please close her eyes, please be an obedient daughter, he bowed his head.

Solanum started laughing, Oh Dad, why aren't you looking? It's so lovely.

She slid off his shoulders, burning him and making him yelp when she moved across his skin. He could feel her standing in front of him, blocking the blaze, and he reached out and grabbed her to pull her close to him, but where he touched her she felt like flame.

The light went out as quickly as it had burst into being. He heard the smoke from the tube hiss to the ceiling, and he reached out again to touch Solanum. Instead of her skin he felt something cold and foreign, and when he opened his eyes he cried out.

He crawled around on his hands and knees. He put his hands on her cold feet and tried to burrow his face as far as he could into the unyielding metal of her body. Above him, Solanum's arms were raised high, but they were not her arms, exactly. They were long and willowy, a grown woman's arms, the kind that were long enough to cradle children and hush the eyes of their sleeping husband. They gleamed harsh gold, as did her smiling face that was hers, and not hers, but a face she had the potential to grow into, stunted into a golden mask. The belly spilling out under the stiff shirt was both his daughter and the home that cradled her. Sarah, he whispered. Solanum. How could he have imagined Solanum was anything but that beautiful bird Sarah so wished for and so resembled when she slept, her head craning away from her body?

the ibex Girl of qumran

When I was a little girl I would beg my grandfather to tell me stories, and he would always tell the one about a girl who lived in a faraway desert, the youngest member of a tribe of tanned shepherds. They were peaceful folk, raising sheep on lofty mountains the color of camel skin, raising children on the banks of the sea of salt. When the great drought came the people were unprepared; they lived morning to night, and never had enough to save up for tomorrow. Many died that season. They prayed to their gods, sacrificed entire flocks, danced on their toes until all the water ran from their bodies, but the rain did not come.

In another life, Grandfather said, I was the daughter of the chief, with the spirit of the desert sanded on my bones. My name was Hessa, the fated one. When my family went hungry, I starved, because I was good, and good meant not eating when others were hungry. My mother was a tall woman who had danced off all her toes, and my father had sent his entire flock into sacrifice, so our family had no more prayers to offer the clear, cruel sky. As Hessa, I slipped out into the night when my parents were asleep and crawled across the desert until sand ripped my skin raw. I travelled farther and farther until I saw an ibex with horns as high as I was tall, made of gold and amber. I followed him across the mountains, and then across the salt sea, where none can drown and none can slake. The ibex drank from the sea and expanded; I drank and my veins went dry. When I could go no farther, I fell to my knees and thought of nothing. The ibex tipped his lovely horns to my head and where they touched my skin I tore apart. Underneath my human leather was a soft ibex kid with silver horns and black eyes. I raised myself on steady legs, bleated my new voice, and went into the rising sun. The next morning, the rain came.

Grandfather told me this story every time I asked, and sometimes when I did not. I grew tired of hearing it and would beg for something new, but each time it was always the drought and the sacrifice.

I'm not Hessa. You made her up, I accused him, and he would always say, Yes, of course, it's just a story.

When I grew up, I tried to find where the story came from. Grandfather was intelligent, but not exactly creative, and I doubted his ability to make it up. When I asked my mother, she only shrugged, and said she had never heard such a bizarre tale. That only made me want to know more, because it was something special between us, a secret that I didn't fully understand except that it was ours. I scoured the library, but it was not in any book of myths or fairy tales. I Googled, and while some results were cartoonish or funny, occasionally pornographic, there were no real leads.

Why do you want to know? he'd ask.

Because it's our story, I would say.

He wouldn't tell me anything, except that the story was meant for me, and that was all there was to it.

When he was seventy-eight, Grandfather suffered a heart attack from twenty years of his dead wife being unable to stop him from eating a dinner of potato chips and sausage four times a week. He survived, barely, and my family watched him with a dire curiosity, waiting for the inevitable, but he was stubborn. He made me put my ear to his chest to prove it beat on tempo, and I had to strain to hear.

On the morning of his eighty-first birthday he tripped over a mound of dirt in his backyard. His hip fractured before he hit the ground, as if his bones were made of sandstone. The doctors told us he wouldn't walk without assistance for the rest of his life, if he walked at all. Then they handed us assisted living brochures, the kind with bemused faces and wrinkled smiles playing endless games of bridge and pinochle on the glossy covers.

I've heard that the older someone is when they go under the anesthesia, the more it screws with the head. When grandfather was coming out of surgery he called my name, sometimes he'd say *Hessa, Hessa,* like a plea, or ask if the whir of the machines around him was rain. I sat next to him for hours, gripping his hand.

If I met her now I think I'd be happy, Grandfather said, his eyes unfocused.

I'm right here, I said, and he gripped my hand and turned his head aside. Then I said, You're not happy? but he was sleeping.

When he was released I stayed away. He stubbornly refused to go into assisted living, so even though I knew he needed help, I went back to my apartment in the city so I wouldn't have to watch him spend minutes on each and every step, or grip the rails in the bathroom. If he died, I wanted to remember him as something more than fragile. When we were younger, he used to let me win at chess, and in the summers he'd dab sunscreen on my nose and chase me around the park, whooping, his arms above his head. I excused myself from family gatherings by telling my mother I had to work. I said I was an important member of the bank. The best auditor they had. I made up business cards that said so.

I claimed work until his next birthday, when I had to attend or risk my mother sending me multiple caps-locked e-mails. For his gift, I had a cane made for him from the horns of some virile ibex and shipped in across the ocean. It cost me a fortune and it was beautiful: bone white and trimmed with gold. Flawless. Usually Grandfather loved my gifts, even when I was five and gave him a haphazard mess of Popsicle sticks and clumpy Elmer's glue and told him it was the Statue of Liberty. Mother had said he was walking better now, and only needed a sturdy cane. It seemed a good gift, but when I put it in his hands he held it away from his body.

Like the girl, I tried to explain. In your story.

He thanked me and put it aside. Later that night, I saw him holding it away from his body, his shoulders hunched up.

After a month of watching him grasp the metal hospital-issued cane, I cashed in half a decade's worth of vacation time and bought two round-trip tickets to Israel, the only place I knew contained a salt sea. Besides my mother, the only person to tell was my rotund and sappy boss. At first he wasn't going to give me the time off, so I lied and said I was half-Jewish on my father's side.

Go, he said, waving his arms like a benediction. If you don't find yourself now when you're young, you'll never get the chance.

Grandfather kissed me on the forehead when I showed him the tickets.

Real ibex, I said. Up close. Cool, right? Like we're a part of the story. And we can see where Hessa ate and slept and played with her family by the shore.

Grandfather laughed and called me his pretty ibex girl, always thinking of others. He said, I hope my tired legs can get me that far. He tapped his cane on his healed hip.

You walk just fine, I said. You're fine.

He limped to his bedroom and packed the smallest bag he owned, which I attributed to him having never travelled outside of the States before. I filled up half my suitcases with extra clothes and things for him.

My mother called and told me not to take him. I listened to her worries and said I was going anyway. I was going to prove he was fine. I hung up on her. Twenty minutes later I received an e-mail:

U THINK TAKING A DYING MAN OVERSEAS
WILL HELP HIM?! UR NUTS!
LOVE, UR MOM
P.S. DONT GET BLOWN UP!!

Grandfather and I flew eleven excruciating hours into Tel Aviv and stood for an additional two in lines at the airport. I asked the stodgy woman at passport control if this was typical and she said yes, tourism booms between conflicts.

I'd made arrangements with my travel guide for us to meet up with a tour agent in Jerusalem to take us wherever we wanted to go. Their prices were exorbitant, but for the supposed services they offered, and considering I knew little of the place beyond when the violence made headlines, I figured it would be worth the cost. They had a cab waiting for us outside the airport. Grandfather pointed out everything on the way, the palm trees, the skyscrapers piercing the neon Tel Aviv sky. He falsetto'd his excitement when we passed camels on the dusty roads, and I asked the driver to slow down so we could watch them walk in their funny, plodding manner.

We arrived in Jerusalem, exhausted from reclining on the plane and sitting in the cab. We found a cheap restaurant that accepted American money and ate chewy falafel with hummus, the only thing we recognized on the menu. Our hotel was located in New Jerusalem, near one of the entrances to the old city. The air smelled like spice and tasted like the cheap metal of coin and sweat. We shared a room with a halfhearted but loud air conditioner. Grandfather fell asleep immediately, but I stayed awake as long as I could to watch him breathe.

In the morning we met our guide, Amir, in the lobby. He was tall, slightly muscular, like a soccer player. He smiled and shook grandfather's hand and asked him how he liked the weather. When he smiled at me I could see all his teeth. He didn't look much older than me, and when I asked it turned out he wasn't, but he swore guiding was his passion, and he had been doing it alongside his father since he could talk.

At my urging, Grandfather told him the story of the ibex girl, but he left out the part where I had been Hessa.

I haven't heard that story, Amir said. But there are many small tribal groups in this country, and they each have their own secrets. If you're looking for the ibex, I can show you.

He took us to a zoo on the edge of Jerusalem. We could have stayed home.

There, he said, pointing to an ibex herd grazing behind bars. Want me to read the sign? he offered, since it was in Hebrew.

I asked Grandfather what he thought, and he said they were very nice, larger than he expected, but he pointed to the zoo map and said could we go see the penguins? Amir explained penguins were not native to this part of the world while Grandfather mimicked their squacks. When we got to the little white myna birds, Amir unhelpfully supplied Grandfather with dirty phrases in Arabic, which they both tried to get the birds to mimic. By the end of the day they were slapping each other's backs and laughing like morons.

For dinner we returned to the hotel, and Grandfather filled a plate from the cafeteria and limped his way back to the room, claiming lethargy and jet lag, something only an excessive amount of sleep could remedy. Amir was on the clock for a few more hours, and because Grandfather kept saying I would only disturb him if I was in the room, Amir and I took to the streets and found a place that served cold Pakistani beer and hot shawarma.

We call this gyro, I told him, holding up the pita.

In the United Kingdom, he said, they call it a doner kebab.

Have you been?

He'd studied history at The University of Kent, about an hour southeast of London.

Ah, I said. Your English is really good.

I drained my beer to wash that sentence back down my throat. Thankfully he smirked, but I knew I couldn't have been more insulting if I was trying, so I asked where we could go to see a real herd of ibex. Preferably wild ones who walked near the Dead Sea. Amir said they were all over the Qumran area, but that I should see the traditional tourist haunts before we left Jerusalem.

He said, What are you going to do after you see the ibex? You take a picture, take an hour to float in the sea. See the Dead Sea Scroll caves. Go to Masada and walk the ruins. Takes an afternoon to see all of it. Not much else down there, unless you like the desert.

We had to see, at Amir's insistence, the traditional places for each major religion: The Wailing Wall, The Temple Mount, The Holy Sepulcher. And the bazaars, to appease the god all religions could agree on, and to whom all Americans specifically wondered at and loved.

We're here for the ibex, I said. And the girl, Hessa.

Amir said, I thought she was made up.

He walked me back to my hotel, even though he was off the clock. In the lobby he hesitated, shifting his weight from leg to leg. I thought he was going to proposition me, and I was thinking of the most politely vicious way to say no.

Instead, he said, Your grandfather is very old. Then he waited.

Okay, I said.

He shook his head. It will be easier for you out in the desert. But your grandfather? He will find it very difficult.

You don't know my grandfather very well, I said.

I wanted to drive out to Qumran the next day, but Amir arrived early for breakfast and cornered Grandfather with sweet coffee and peach yogurt and stories about the Sepulcher. Grandfather said he wanted to see it.

But we came to see the ibex, I said. And you're not Christian.

It's historical, he said. We can see the ibex tomorrow.

We went into the old city. Two armed guards looked bored as we walked by. They made me feel uncomfortable, or the guns strapped to their sides did, so I lowered my head and avoided eye contact. Amir waved to them, and then Grandfather did, too.

The roads were uneven and streets crowded with laughing children and quick-eyed shopkeepers. And Americans with American cameras.

I almost lost Grandfather to several shopkeepers as every time they said they had a deal or a bargain, or called him friend, he would stop and listen, inspect the goods as if we needed a menorah or a replicate crown of thorns. Amir haggled for a gray pashmina and draped it around my bare shoulders.

You need to cover up in the holy places, he said as I protested. He added, It matches your eyes.

I spent the entire time walking through the church thinking about the pashmina and listening to Amir whisper the history of each nook and work of art.

Did you know, he said as we watched an Armenian woman prostrate herself before an image of the Virgin behind glass, the Sepulcher is a separated whole. He gestured to the far ends of the church. He said, Everyone owns a part of it. Catholics, Armenians, Eastern Orthodox. It's been claimed and lost and reclaimed many times.

The woman began murmuring in her language, and held a damp handkerchief to her eyes. Amir continued, The main entrance to the church is locked by these two huge wooden doors. Would you like to guess who holds the key?

Grandfather guessed the Catholics. I watched the women shake her head back and forth. She breathed in trembling gulps. A man in all black put his finger to his lips and made a wet shushing noise at her.

Two Muslim families, Amir said. Since the time of Saladin. One family locks up at night, and another opens it in the morning.

The woman didn't quiet herself. She put her head down onto her lace-covered chest and grasped at her heart, the icons on her rings and around her wrist catching the light. The men left me to go watch the Orthodox and Franciscan prayer services, but I stayed and watched her put her hands close to the glass, never touching, but so obviously longing to do so. I thought she was the most holy thing in the place, and I wondered what it would be like to be her, even if she was sad and

I couldn't understand why. What I wouldn't do for that intangible sense of belonging, even if belonging was painful.

After, we went to the Western Wall. I had no real interest—a wall is a wall—but Grandfather went up and slipped a hastily written prayer between the cracks. I asked him what he wrote, but he said it wouldn't come true if he told me. I said I didn't think God worked like fountains or birthday candles, but he said there was a lot I didn't know.

The next day I tried to get grandfather and Amir to go to Qumran, but Amir waved a paper fan in front of grandfather and himself and claimed it was too hot. Grandfather held out his arms and shook them. Look, I'm sweating sitting down, he said.

The car is air conditioned, I said, but they were both staring at me, and I knew we weren't going to Qumran that day.

We did go to the Mount of Olives to see the panoramic view of the city. I took pictures of Grandfather doing funny balancing acts with his cane, and he took a picture of me sitting on the ledge with the Dome of the Rock behind me. He told Amir to come sit in the picture with me, and Amir draped his arm around my shoulder and made the peace sign.

We ate a light lunch of vegetable salads and decided to go shopping between seeing some of the smaller sights; parts of the old wall and the convenient stations of the Cross. I easily acquiesced since I had to get my mother something to make up for not answering her e-mails of increasing font size. I was looking at a gold statue of a bird when a street peddler approached me. He had hundreds of cheap plastic necklaces draped around his neck and both his arms. He shoved a choker of fake amethysts into my hand. I told him, no thank you, and tried to give it back.

You are beautiful, he said out of nowhere. No charge. No charge. It is for you. You smile, now?

I didn't know what else to do, so I awkwardly smiled and thanked him.

He stood closer to me. Do you have a man?

I was stunned into truth, and so I said I didn't.

I will marry you, he said and thrust his arms out, the beads jangling, like a bird of paradise with its plumage on display for a mate.

Oh, I said. Thank you?

I will make a very good husband, he continued. I will take care of you.

Just when I was afraid I had accidentally entered into a vow of matrimony, Amir put his hand on my shoulder and said something in Arabic to the peddler. The man gave me a sad smile and reached his hand out. I thought he wanted the necklace back, but instead he took my hand and shook it. He said I should smile more. He nodded to Amir one more time, then went over to a group of Japanese tourists and waved his necklaces in front of them.

What did you say to him? I asked.

Amir grinned. I told him you couldn't marry him because you were going to marry me.

He walked ahead of me to where Grandfather was waiting, leaning on his cane, grinning at us.

I did my best to ignore Amir for the rest of the day, and gave one-word answers whenever I had to speak. Amir asked if I wanted to out with him that night, experience some of the Israeli nightlife. I considered it, but I thought what if Grandfather stopped breathing in the middle of the night, or needed a glass of water with an aspirin? I said no. Grandfather looked more disappointed than Amir.

He's a nice boy, Grandfather said when we in our hotel room, getting ready for bed.

You can't be serious, Grandpa.

He shrugged. Maybe. You should have fun. You're young. When's the last time you went out with a man?

I don't have time for a man, I snapped. I'm too busy worrying about you.

Grandfather sat on the bed and rolled his cane between his hands.

I slammed the door to the bathroom and took a lukewarm shower. I tried to make it hot, I wanted to scald myself, but it only reached tepid. When I came out, grandfather was already in his bed, faking sleep. He usually snored. I pinned my hair up and crawled into my bed, turned off the light. We lay without moving.

It isn't a good thing, Grandfather started. I jerked but didn't say anything. I heard him shift his weight around in the bed, his bones creak, and the muffled sound of pain. I closed my eyes when I heard him cough.

It is not good to be Hessa, he said, finally. She's such a serious girl. She never laughs in that story, you know? All she does is sacrifice herself for drops of water.

I felt a sickly emotion twist behind my eyes, so I rolled my face onto my pillow. She had to. Else she would have dehydrated and died. They all would have.

I suppose you're right, he said.

I clutched my hands under my head and asked, Where did you hear the story?

I heard him turn. I don't know, he said. Sometimes you hear things and you don't remember where they came from. But you, even when you were young, you always reminded me of that girl.

I didn't know what to say. It seemed anticlimactic and awful and typical all at once. After a while I heard him begin to snore.

In the morning I stayed in bed and thought about going home early. By the time I got up and went downstairs, Grandfather and Amir had already started eating breakfast. I ordered coffee with milk and went to fill a plate with oatmeal and fruit from the buffet line. Amir came up next to me and loaded his plate with fish and eggs.

We will go to Qumran today, he said, helping me pick out the cantaloupe from the medley. But your grandfather might not find it very comfortable. The Dead Sea is the lowest point on Earth. The pressure there, he made a low whistle. It's pretty bad.

I snuck a glance at my grandfather. He was making exaggerated gestures with his hands to young, giggly waitress, his cane behind his back, out of sight.

He'll be fine, I said.

The drive to Qumran was quiet and smooth and not very long. Israel is surprisingly small for all you hear about it; it's only about the size of Rhode Island. The air conditioning was blasting on high and sweat poured down my back. I felt lightheaded from the pressure, and Grandfather rested his head on the window. I shook his arm and pointed out the land as it matched the story. The camel-skinned mountains, the shepherds lazily walking their sheep or goats across the sand.

They are Bedouin shepherds, Amir explained. Did you know, they have a thousand words for death, and only one for birth.

Grandfather pressed his face to the car window. He asked, Why is that?

To the people in these parts, birth is simple, uncomplicated. It is the same word for joy. But death comes swift, like the storm, and requires more language to explain than we can make up.

I knew he was talking to me. Is that true, I asked. I fished out my suntan lotion and applied it to my arms in what I hoped was a neutral gesture. A thousand words?

Amir grinned at me. You can ask them.

Some of the encampments we passed were made of mismatched sheet metal with doorways of thin blankets. I saw groups of children, barefoot, dirty, kicking a ball or chasing one another down the sand hills. There was a woman sitting on an overturned bucket, stitching a young girl's faded yellow dress.

Amir stopped the car on the side of the road where a band of shepherds were sitting under a grove of thin trees, eating lunch, surrounded by a herd of goats. They all wore long, white robes that covered their entire bodies. I wondered how they didn't keel over from heatstroke. I was drenched in sweat. My ears were clogged from the pressure, and

I worked my jaw trying to loosen it while Amir talked with the shepherds. I handed grandfather a water bottle, which he dumped over his head. I wanted to do the same, but I was wearing a white tank.

One of the shepherds invited us to share the meal, and we all sat down. I took as little as possible, but Grandfather and Amir made up for it by taking far too much.

They're poor, I whispered in Grandfather's ear.

They also understand English, Amir said out of the side of his mouth.

The shepherds smirked at me. I lowered my head and ate a piece of carrot as slowly as I could.

We were asked to tell the story of Hessa. Amir said if anyone knew it would be the Bedouins, who still kept their histories and lessons alive by whispering stories in their children's ears. I was too embarrassed to talk, so Grandfather told it to them.

Again he left out the part where I was Hessa, but this time I did not mind. I didn't want any attention. When Grandfather finished, the shepherds looked at one another and started to speak rapidly in their language. Then one addressed Amir for a long time.

They have heard a similar version, Amir said. But it differs. The girl turned into an ibex, but instead of going off, she came back to the village. Her father did not recognize her and, mad with hunger, he tore her apart and ate her. Amir grimaced. Then the rain came.

I gaped in horror. I expected Grandfather to be equally indignant, but he was nodding his head and looking at me. Amir interjected with more Arabic, and the shepherds started to talk amongst themselves in low murmurs. One of them, who I would guess was the oldest from his leathery, wrinkled face, pointed to a low mountain in the East.

They are saying we should look over there. The Ibex run the hills and mountains.

We thanked them for their help and for the lunch. I wanted to give them money, but Amir said they were too proud to accept charity. I ignored him and tried to give it to them anyway. One of them took the wad of bills and handed me a baby goat. They laughed when I tried to give it back, and the little thing squirmed so much I dumped it in the backseat of the car.

Grandfather sat with it in the back, petting it and cupping bottled water for it to drink.

For pity's sake, I said. Don't get attached. We can't bring it back with us.

It was a quick drive to the mountain. When we reached the base, Grandfather used his belt to make a short leash. Unfortunate, as I was hoping the damned goat would run away. Amir went up ahead of us to make sure we could climb with relative ease. Grandfather leaned on his cane and me, and I dragged the goat behind us. It was an easy climb. There were plenty of places for us to steady ourselves, and the incline wasn't bad. I wondered if this entire land was made for people to walk on and look at and take a picture and then forget about it. Maybe that's why the people kept on doing all sorts of mad things around here, not just for politics or religion or cultural divides, but a mass subconscious desire not to be lost in some cheap airport souvenir book.

Partway up were several caves. They weren't very large, but the three of us and the goat could fit comfortably in them. From the entrance I could see the banks of the Dead Sea, clear and stagnant.

This is cool, I said. I smiled and walked around, putting my hands on the wall and enjoying the feeling of stone and history. Just think about all the stuff that happened here, I said, rather unaware if anything of note had ever happened in this part of the country. Let's keep going. Hessa's parents probably would have lived at the top.

Amir avoided my eyes when I looked for support.

I'm tired, Grandfather said. He held his hospital cane in one hand and made a half-hearted motion at the goat with the other. So is little Hessa here. Let's rest a while.

I faltered. You named the goat?

Grandfather slid down a wall and sat, hunched into himself. It's just a story. He said "story" like it was a throwaway. It's just rain. It's just a wound.

I felt ill.

It's your story, I said slowly. When neither of them looked at me, I grunted, I came all this way for you.

I looked down at him and saw a tired old man clutching a dusty metal cane. He wouldn't meet my eyes. I wanted to hug him and hit him.

Amir pulled out a cigarette and lit it up. When Grandfather coughed, I smacked it out of his mouth.

The hell do you think you're doing! I shouted. You're going to make him sick!

Both of them stared at me. My hands trembled with a desire to hurt. I wanted to cry, but I'd be damned if I'd let them see me do it. With as much dignity as I could muster, I raised my head and marched out of the cave. I had no idea where I was going, and I could hear both of their voices behind me, but I kept towards the high path.

I didn't get far, the pressure and heat winded me, and beyond that I had never been much for exercise. I leaned against the rough path and looked out into the distance at the desert. I could see a man with a flock of sheep walking along the banks of the sea. What a strange life these people must live, to wake up to a body of water where they could not drink or drown. Did they feel blessed or cheated by such a strange, natural miracle?

I saw Amir coming up towards me. I wouldn't look at him. He made like he wanted to say something, but then shrugged and stood next to me. For a while we were silent, but then he started to hum a tune I didn't recognize.

What do you want? I finally said.

You know, the people here have a saying—

I don't want to hear it, Amir.

He put his hands up in a gesture of peace. They say it brings madness to deny the inevitable. Your grandfather. He is dying.

I pulled at the skin near my wrist with my nails. He is not dying, I said. And what do you know? You're a tour guide.

Amir shook his head.

I raised my hand, fully prepared to hit him and knock those words out of his mouth and head. I could tell he knew I would hit him, and he had enough time to react, but he did not. That, too, made me angry. I slapped his face. Then I slapped him again. And again. It felt good to hurt him. I wanted to continue, to slap all thoughts of grandfather and me out of his head, but he grabbed my hands and held them. Then he stared at my mouth, and I knew with excruciating predictability that he wanted to kiss me. I imagined taking my clothes off for him, watching him take his clothes off for me, the combination of our nudity. I put my arms around his neck and mashed my lips on his. He stumbled back and grabbed my hips to hold me steady. He tasted nice, like soap and salt.

A stunted bleat near my legs pulled me away from the embrace. The damn goat, with grandfather's belt trailing after it like an extended tail. I pushed Amir away and started to run back down, my head feeling like it might rupture. I heard Amir yell something about catching the goat, but I was running and tripping down the mountain with a sure-footedness born of panic.

Grandfather was where I had left him, leaning against the wall. With effort, he raised his head and smiled at me. She got away from me, he said.

I crumbled down next to him and rested my head on his shoulder. I'm sorry, I said. I wanted you to be happy.

You don't know what you want, he said.

On impulse I grabbed his hand and held it up to my face. I traced the grooves of his hand, the raised veins, the thin white scar at the base of his thumb, just as I had done when I was a child. And, like when I was a child, he took my hand in his and asked if I wanted to hear a story.

When I said yes, he sighed out all the breath in him.

He began: Once, there was a young girl who lived in a nearby place, who loved her family, and went into the desert to find water, or food, or a god on four legs. By the time he reached Hessa's disfigurement his voice had grown dry and weak, so I took over the narrative. When I said the rain had come, we both looked outside at the clear sky.

I squeezed my eyes shut and whispered, You're not going to leave me, are you, Grandpa?

He brought my hand to his lips and kissed me. No, he said. Not until you're no longer a silly little girl in a story.

I kissed Amir, I said, wanting him to be happy with me. I said, Hessa wouldn't have done that.

He squeezed my hand. No, she wouldn't have.

The sun was beginning to move towards the west, though it would be several hours before night. I wondered where Amir was. When I began to disentangle our hands, I saw a large shadow stretched across our legs. I thought it was Amir come back with the goat. But this was not Amir. I thought my eyes were tricking me. Perhaps hallucinating from the heat. I gently prodded my grandfather. Grandpa, look. Look.

It was different than the strong males in the herd we had seen at the zoo. Different, and familiar, like I had wished it into tangibility. It seemed so tall, its legs so long that if it walked as a man it would be a giant. Its horns were thicker than my arm, curled, adorned with the touch and shimmer of sunlight.

Tentative, I approached the beast on my hands and knees, whispering cooing nonsense so it wouldn't bolt. It moved its heavy head and the glare of the sun hit me full on. The shadow of its horns vivisected me down the middle. I trembled before it. Dumbfounded, I watched it come closer to us, its legs impossibly long and sure, its calves like fists, its haunches covered in dirty, matted fur. I searched its eyes for a sign of what it wanted, but they were gray and dull, lifeless. The beast was blind. Even so, it knew its path, and its steps were sure.

It moved towards grandfather with a precise grace, like the sword of Damocles cut from its hair-string. Fear and instinct drove me in front of him, and I threw my arms out like a willing Isaac. Get out of here, I said. The strange beast raised its head and bellowed. It bared rotting, black teeth so close to my face I could smell its sour breath. Maggots squirmed between its molars. It lowered its mighty head to mine and I had to close my eyes.

And then my grandfather said, Oh, isn't it beautiful? Isn't it wonderful? and I wondered if we saw the same thing.

When its horns touched me, I felt and saw the image of the young ibex—Hessa, of course—with her supple and weak legs. And her eyes, not the matte black of an animal, but my own blue intellect in an animal face. On my head were not horns, but a heavy crown of silver starlight.

This was me, and this was not me. I felt bile rising up to the back of my throat when I imagined myself as an animal, even one so blessed as that. In all my life I had never felt particularly close to my human skin, but now I wanted it, wanted to glue and brand it to myself. I thrashed out at this satyr face that was mine and not, wanting only to see it destroyed, burned at a spit, dissected of fur and hoof until my real self was pulled out from underneath.

I cried out, No. No. No. And then the image was gone, and there was nothing before me. I felt my eyes and the top of my head, ran my human fingers across my stomach to see if there was any indication of change, in case the process of transformation was painless, or numbing. But I was whole, as whole as I ever was.

I turned to my grandfather with joy. I'd saved us both, and nothing was lost.

Grandfather looked at me with his quiet smile, and then he was my grandfather no more. He leaned over and fell onto his hands like a child playing animal. His skin, already thinned with age, whitened and shone like loose leaf paper at the edges: his knee, his elbows, his cheekbones.

Then he split apart. Underneath was no blood or bone, but tufts of black hair, like on the heads of newborn birds.

His head tore in two. Clean down the middle. There was no mess, like he had taken off the costume of this life as man. And under that human mask there was—could there be anything else?—a small ibex with black eyes and black fur, two bumps of silver at the top of its head, pinpoints of beauty.

He shook off the old body easily; it was like it had never been his at all. His new fur glistened with a birthing dew, clean and sweet. He approached me and lowered his head. I was too afraid to touch him, so he butted against my hand. How different this newness felt, slick and sharp, soft and dull, like he was made of contradiction. I grabbed at his feet and held him to the ground, but there was little to hold onto, and he slid from my grasp.

The golden ibex bellowed again, but softer this time, almost gentle. They spoke in their language, the little one bleating high pitched, all joy. They turned from me and, because I dared not follow, I called out for them to stop. They paid me no heed, too entranced in their own song and dance. Then they faded, one second raising their hoofs and bellowing from their throats, and then gone, like they had never been there at all.

I met Amir at the entrance to the cave. Is your grandfather all right? he asked. He was carrying the damn goat in his arms, cuddled to his chest.

Is it going to rain tonight? I said. Or, tomorrow?

Amir tried to look behind me into the cave, but I grabbed his arm. He said the rain would not come for another month, at least. It's the dry season. But I strained my eyes beyond him at the looming sky. I wondered how I ever thought such an expansive thing was clear. There was light and shadows, so many colors, tumbling together in a dance until the inevitable happened, and it fell all around us.

Beasts

When I was only up to her knee, my Gran-ma-ma would bend down and whisper her stories into the curls of my hair. Each one was similar to the one she told before: always a young girl went into the forest before her first bleeding, always she ran with her clothes falling off of her, torn apart by the force of her legs slapping the earth, and always at the end she was gobbled up by a beast with teeth as thick as my arm. When she spoke of her beloved rough beast, the paper-thin skin on her fingers and hands stretched and fluttered. Her wrinkled cheeks flushed, and her eyes turned bright.

But why must it always be a man-beast? my mother said, lighting her pipe which at one time been my grandfather's. Mother, in a fit of young temper, had taken the pipe, lit, from Grandfather's frosty lips and plopped it in her own. Within the year she had appropriated all his pipes in a similar manner. She even plucked his last, the thin black one he quietly smoked in the corner, from his crooked hands when he died. But the first one was always her favorite, because it was his largest and could hold the most tobacco.

She wrapped her lips around the small end and furiously sucked, her cheeks expanding and shrinking with the effort. She said, I thought the bitches of the forest did all the work. Gran-ma-ma shushed her with a quick jerk of her hand.

It's always been a man-beast, she scoffed, her throat rioting up into a hack. Can't tell the story right, she said, spitting into the cold hearth, unless you tell it like it's always been told. Oh, put that out! It bothers my throat.

Mother moved to the window. When Gran-ma-ma went back to her house in the middle of the forest, my father accompanied her. She did not need an escort, she knew her way, but she was prone to tripping and breaking her glass-bone hips. When she was past the tree line, my mother sat me at the table and told me, her voice all reason, that if I ever met a man-beast in the forest I should simply gut him and be done with it.

But what if he is a kind man-beast? I asked. What if—She tapped her pipe on the table. There is no such thing. All man-beasts will eat you, no, destroy you, if you give them half a chance. My mother was optimistic like that.

One day, my father was out gathering berries to make his daily fruit pastry. I'd never seen nor tasted anything more delightful than the rows of tarts, cakes, pies, and sweet buns that adorned our sills, our counters, our tables, and when finished with this task, my mother would take his berry-stained fingers to her lips and wrap her tongue around his plump digits, saying what a good boy he was. Mother called out to him from the window that she wanted blueberries, for a pie, then puffed, puffed, puffed. You should visit your grandmother, she told me. I haven't heard from her in days. She's probably got the flu again and hasn't deemed us worthy of a letter.

But, Mummy, I said, Gran-ma-ma's hand cramps up.

Pah! My mother spat in the flowerpot on the sill.

In spite of my complaints, Mother had packed a large, wicker basket of day-old fruit tarts, a bit of hard, black bread, cheese, and a bottle of wine. As she packed that, wrapping the heavy bottle in a checked cloth, she told me I had better not drink any.

But it's bad for Gran-ma-ma! I said.

Pish posh, said Mother. It might give the old hag a thrill.

I stuck my finger in the strawberry tart for a taste, but my mother slapped my hand before I made it to my mouth. I glared at her. Mummy, I said, shouldn't I bring medicine? What if Gran-ma-ma really is sick?

My mother shushed me. She said, Your grandmother wouldn't take it unless she dug it out of the ground herself. If she's ill, put a warm cloth on her forehead and hold her hand until she's better. She wrapped me in my red wool cloak with the pointed hood that I'd gotten from Gran-ma-ma as a birthday gift years ago, and stuck a box of ammunition for Gran-ma-ma's shotgun in the pocket. I did not tell her the bullets were unnecessary; Gran-ma-ma had never touched the thing after politely letting Mother show her how to use it. She also handed me her sharpest hunting knife—her favorite for gutting rabbits. Remember to twist it, she said, placing the handle in my hand. You need to really get it in there and twist it if you want to really do some damage, sweetheart.

I took off for the forest, passing my father on the way. He gave me a dazed good-bye, his eyes fixed on his basket of fruit.

The path to get to Gran-ma-ma's is lovely. It was the end of summer, so the trees were slowly beginning their beautiful rot. There were tinges of yellow on the greens, and the wind carried the scent of sweet decay, like a ripe apple just about to turn.

There was always a sense of calm danger in the forest, like you were forever walking on the edge of a breaking dam. One wrong move, or perhaps even stupid chance, and your fortune would flip and the rushing waves of animal jaws would devour you whole. Gran-ma-ma always said that there were demons and spirits in the forest and once, long ago, people would revere the ancient ones with blood-rites and strange dancing, but Mother always brushed Gran-ma-ma aside, telling her to stop telling such ridiculous tales.

After a while, I began to notice that the forest grew still the more I entered its winding body. The birds stopped their bell-like twittering, the crickets ceased rubbing their musical thighs. Even the leaves were silent. Even though I had only recently begun to bleed, and only recently have begun to know things, I recognized the archaic, intrinsic indication of danger, of change. The fine peach fuzz stood up on my neck, and I felt my less-than-musical thighs quiver in expectation.

I saw him.

He was large, feral, and strange; a black figure with yellow, glowing eyes, his long teeth a sparkling gleam, while his rough, red tongue ran its wet length across his lips. And his lips, easily pulled back, easily shut, with a dash of red—blood?—by the dark bead of his nose. Had he just eaten some young, pale deer that could not jump from his jaw in time? Or perhaps some white rabbit corpse lay not a few feet from me, its own blood staining its fur, its eyes trained, helpless and wide, toward inevitability. But this beast was lean, almost starved, and when he stepped closer I saw the blood at his lip was black with age. Likely, he thought me an offering to his hunger.

I grasped Mother's gouging knife with a trembling hand in the basket, ready to strike if he moved quickly. But he did not jump at me, nor make any movement that seemed violent. Instead, he stared at me with what I thought was amusement. I felt very foolish. I let the hilt of the blade go, and it tumbled to the bottom of the basket.

The wolf lowered his head and approached me. I was nervous at his large form. He looked like he would tower over me if he went on hind-legs like a man. I dared not move. He walked around me with his body so close that I could feel the tips of his fur, rough and matted, against my hand, or brushing my legs. I shivered and squirmed when I thought I felt his long tooth slide across my arm but was too terrified to look down to be sure. A growl escaped his throat, but it was soft and drawn out, a sigh of pleasure.

When he did not bite me, I grew to enjoy the feel of him close to me, his heat and soft panting just by my thighs. He continued his slow circle and I felt bold enough to reach my fingers out and brush them, as lightly as I could, on his thick-furred back.

Quicker than I could retract my hand, the wolf grabbed hold of my wrist in his teeth and bit down hard enough to leave nasty red imprints, but did not break the skin. I fell to my knees, and he shook my hand in his sharp maw. I cried out, Oh, please, oh please, I didn't mean it! I won't touch you again!

This seemed to calm the beast, for with one final shake he released my hand, and instead took to sniffing me. He was most enraptured at the scent where my skin bore the mark of his teeth. As for myself, I felt calm under his attentions, assured that I would remain safe so long as I did not touch him.

When I felt his rough tongue run across my neck, I did not breathe.

After a while, the beast huffed and turned his back to me. When I saw that he was making to leave, I felt a coldness touch my legs, my neck, and my stomach. I was afraid of him, but I did not want him to go. I called out, I am going to my Gran-ma-ma's house in the middle of the forest. She's probably very sick, you see.

The wolf did not turn to face me, but he stopped moving. His ear twitched.

I wouldn't mind seeing you again, if you want, I said. You'd need only follow the road.

The wolf made a snorting noise and was gone. I clasped my hands and hoped I would see him again.

I arrived at Gran-ma-ma's house just before sundown, hours after my strange encounter with the wolf.

I saw that something was wrong. The front door was open and I could hear strange noises inside, so strange I could not even begin to describe them. I went to the window and snuck up to it as quietly as I could. I peeped in and saw Gran-ma-ma's prone form laid out in bed. She was wearing the blue and white lace bonnet and nightgown my mother detests but which Gran-ma-ma treasured. I held my breath when I saw the wolf step up onto the bed. He was careful to step on the edges of her body. Her nightgown sank into the covers under his paws.

I could hear Gran-ma-ma's breathing begin to grow quick and deep, like the heavy panting our dog used to make before Mother put the hollow end of the shotgun in his face. The wolf seemed taken aback at this, because his paw visibly shook, and he would place it down on the comforter and retract it in twitches. Is that you? came Gran-ma-ma's wavering voice, quiet and earnest. I've waited for you. Did you know I've waited for you?

She gave out a low, pitiful wail, like the caterwauling of a wretched cat in the peak of its estrus.

The wolf's soft ears flattened and he lowered his head, as if asking for forgiveness. The beast opened his slick jaws, and each shiny pointed tooth was visible. I was afraid for Gran-ma-ma, and the feeble warning was about to issue from my mouth when the beast drew out his long, red tongue, and ran it slowly up her neck, ending on her pale, thin lips. Gran-ma-ma's breathing came out in erratic huffs, as if she couldn't get enough air into her lungs, and then she released a high pitched whine, like the one my father makes at night sometimes, accompanied by my mother's heavy grunts.

What a sweet tongue you have! she said.

I was enthralled. I imagined that heavy tongue running across my own sensitive neck again, or my lips. Perhaps even my tongue would dart out, quick and shy, and meet his lips, or his fuzzy snout.

In the midst of my fantasy, I almost did not notice the wolf cringing back from my Gran-ma-ma. His soft whine filled my ears, and I felt pity for the dumb beast when he began to lightly paw at Gran-ma-ma's still form.

Her eyes were dull. Her toothy smile was adoring and stuck. My stomach tightened like when I wore the corset Gran-ma-ma gave me to wear one spring before my mother expressly forbade it. I felt like vomiting. The wolf, skittish by his own realization, looked as if he would bolt. I cannot really explain it, but I did not want the wolf to leave. Quick as I could, I slammed Gran-ma-ma's only window shut. The beast petrified still at the bang. He growled and pulled back his lips to show those trembling, vicious teeth. I ran to the door, shouting loudly as I did. The trick worked, for the wolf, terrified at the screams and bellows backed up to the dead fireplace and hid best as he could in the nook.

When I'd entered the house, making sure to lock the door behind me, the wolf seemed confused. His sharp teeth were weary. Without making any sudden movements, I put the basket on the ground and raised my hands in supplication, palms outward. The wolf lowered his head, but his teeth and eyes glowed in the fading light.

I mean you no harm, I said quietly. I only thought that you'd like to stay a little longer. Must you leave so soon? The forest is cold at night, and it is very warm here.

The wolf made a vicious noise, like rocks grinding in his throat, and moved to the back wall. I knew he wanted to escape, but I could not allow this. After all, the beast had come for me. I had asked him to come. It was not fair that Gran-ma-ma should be the only one to enjoy him.

I indicated the basket. Would you care for something to eat? I've packed cheese and cakes for my Gran-ma-ma ....

I looked to her still body, and I hoped the wolf understood that she would not need them anymore. The wolf paced back and forth, nails clicking on the wood floor.

Perhaps you'd like some wine? I bet you've never tried wine before, I said. Slowly, very slowly, for the wolf was watching, I reached down and picked up the bottle of wine and showed it to him. He seemed interested in it, so with my eyes on him and his eyes on me, I went to the cabinet and took out one of Gran-ma-ma's breakfast bowls. I poured half the bottle in the bowl and set it on the floor.

Come now, it's safe. And very tasty. I knelt down and dipped my fingers in the wine and brought them to my lips. It's just like the blood of a rabbit, I said.

I pushed the bowl at him and moved away. Tentatively, the beast made his way. He growled at me, and so I went on my knees and held up my hands to show there were no tricks. His tongue darted out and tasted the wine. He must have liked the taste, or really believed it to be blood, for he began to lap it up. He got his whole snout in that bowl, and when he pulled his head out the dried blood by his nose was gone, replaced with the lighter, thinner wine. When he had finished the bowl, I was unsurprised to watch him stumble on wobbly legs to the foot of the bed and collapse. I quickly went to work.

Using some of the rope Gran-ma-ma used to bind lumber together, I tied a tight collar around his thin neck, and knotted the loose end to the bed, silently thanking my Gran-ma-ma for having had it nailed to the floor. With another bit of rope I tied a sloppy muzzle around his snout to keep him from snapping at me when he woke. Pleased, I brushed his coat. It was rough and warm. I could even feel the strong pulse of his heart through the thick skin. I lay my head down on his stomach and rested.

I awoke to a wet growl in my ear and my head thumping on the floor as the wolf moved out from under me and stood. There was never such a sight as that animal yanking and wrenching at the rope. He was like a bird throwing itself at the bars of his cage, or the fox gnawing at his leg in the steel trap. I was enraptured. The fullness of his rage and power struggling against such little thin strips of rope made my stomach clench. I salivated when the ropes held. I wanted to run up to him and throw myself on him, to rub my body against his as he struggled, to bring some of that passion into me.

It was painfully beautiful to see his neck and snout rubbed raw by the course twines and to hear his grunts and groans turn to breathy whines, but I steeled myself from pity. It was the only way to keep him.

When he'd tired himself out, lying prostrate on the floor and following me with his cold, yellow eyes, I took stock of the house. I had forgotten all about poor Gran-ma-ma with the business of the wolf and looked with curiosity on her now. She looked peaceful with that queer smile still gracing her face, her wide eyes blank as parchment. With my mother's determination in me, I went about covering her body with the blanket. After, I did not know what else to do with her. There was no way I could carry her outside and bury her all by myself, though I did consider getting some flowers to lay on her. But that seemed too sentimental. It wasn't like she'd know to appreciate them anyhow.

The wolf did not move the entire time I strutted around the house, and I found myself admiring his bound physique more often than not. What was missing from his bones was meat, and so I tried to tempt him with the foods Mother had packed, but he would have none of it. I spoke very softly, as one would speak to a child, and told him how yummy the bread and cheese and tarts were, but he would not take it. He only turned his head away or swiped at me with his paws.

As the days drew on the wolf grew more and more haggard. I could only get him to drink water, and even then I had to wrestle him down and open his jaws as far as the rope would allow with my hands and funnel the liquid down. This task grew easier as time passed and his strength diminished. But Gran-ma-ma had begun to reek. I had no idea that the body began to decay so quickly, but the smell, at first just a faint whiff of rot, soon grew unbearable. I did not think I could lift her outside and bury her on my own. There had to be another way.

I wrote to my mother and told her that Gran-ma-ma had passed. I cried over the letter. I wrote that I would take care of her, and there was no reason for her and my father to make the trip. They had a garden to take care of, a house to run, and I was but a girl without husband or child, and so had no one to care for.

My mother wrote back: Do what you must. Keep the gun close to you when you bury her. You remember how to load it, don't you sweetheart? Bullets in. Keep the safety off. Do not hesitate.

With trembling fingers I removed the muzzle from the beast. Thinking he would snap at me, I backed away, but the most he did was stretch his jaw. It made a terrible cracking noise, like bones snapping. Untying the leash from the bed, I tugged at him until he stood up and followed. I made him climb on the bed by slapping the mattress, as one would with a dog. Uncovering Gran-ma-ma and trying not to look at her sunken cheeks and rotting eyes, I lifted her hand to his mouth.

Gran-ma-ma would have wanted it this way.

Several hours later he vomited her up.

I soothed his growling stomach by feeding him soft breads and fruit and milk. After a few half-hearted attempts at resisting he lowered his mouth to my hand and ate in a daze. His eyes became dull and glossy, like the doll's eyes that Gran-ma-ma had given me when I was a girl. I'm not even sure he knew what he was eating.

I knew he would have preferred dead flesh, so I attempted to get him meat by trapping rabbits like Mother had shown me how to do with snares of wire or rope. I always cooked the meat before I gave it to the wolf, and he would knock it about with his paws and whine when it flopped on the floor. Still, he did eat it.

Soon he grew healthier, and there was a definite pudginess to him. His coat grew shiny each time I brushed him with Gran-ma-ma's comb. He never resisted when I put my hands through his fur, which I confess I did often. Eventually I was able to leave the muzzle off his face, and even the leash from around his throat when I wasn't off in the forest hunting. Whenever I came back he was always the same: still where I left him, staring at the dancing fire in the hearth, his body in a chair, his head and front paws prostrate on the table.

I would like to have said that I was happy, but I was not. I tried to plead with him, I burrowed myself into his soft fur and cried, I offered my arm to him and told him he could bite me if he wanted to, rip me to shreds and eat me as a sacrifice to his once-great-might, but he just looked away or rolled over onto his side so I could put my head on his growing belly to sleep.

And though he was warm and soft, his dull eyes horrified me. There was a nothingness in those dark, wide spheres and oh, what large eyes he had! I could feel myself being drawn into them, helpless in an ever-widening recess.

The only thing to do was to let him go. Perhaps if he were back in the forest he would be as he was, as I wanted him to be. When I cut his leash with Mother's knife and threw the door open the damn thing just sat there staring at the greenery beyond the door like something he once might have known, which was now foreign to him, and strange.

When he would not leave, I took the rifle Mother had given Granma-ma and shot him.

the Romantic Agony of Lemon Head

She lived among an orchard of lemon trees with her father. At spring's beginning she would pick unripe fruit from the branches and squeeze the juice of five hundred and seven lemons—it always had to be five hundred and seven, carefully picked and carefully counted out—into her hair and skin so that she shined and lost all color and was almost translucent. In the summer she smelled of sweet rot, and everywhere she went all who smelled her would stop and stare and want.

At first, her father thought it wonderful for his daughter to smell so sweet and have skin so smooth and burned away; it was fine as paper silk. All the village boys—and maybe some of the less hoity-toity dandies—would come on bended knee before him and ask for her hand. Though all the boys had entered her room with their nostrils flared and their lungs rapidly inflating, they would get near her pale form and their faces would fall, their noses would close up, and they'd say thank you kindly but no thank you and be on their way.

Her father began to worry that she might never get married, and her mother was dead so there was no asking her. Instead he dusted off the old texts, *Raising Lilith into Eve*, *Overcoming Ophelia*, and *Girls Will Be Girls—Uh Oh!* According to these books she was practically an old spinster already—almost sixteen!—and it was not as if she could do any sort of lucrative craft like weaving or playing the harp or keeping the toilet clean since she spent so much time among the orchard picking lemons and hand squeezing them into her morning, midday, after-dinner, and midnight baths. The books were very particular about lucratively attracting men.

So he began to spy on her to see what was wrong that turned so many men away. He cut a bite-sized hole in the bathroom wall and followed her with his eye, but nothing seemed out of the ordinary, though when she squeezed the lemons in her dainty hands the juice would sometimes spray into his exposed eye and he would cry all night.

Wouldn't you like a husband? he would ask, holding her pale hand in his own while she soaked in lemony bubbles. He showed her pictures of girls with young men from the books. The girls in the pictures seemed to float wherever they went when their hands were held by a young man.

She looked at him as if she could not fathom what he was talking about, but she nodded and said, I suppose, in an airy way, and when he looked sad she said, OK.

But he wanted the help of an expert, so he called on Yadda Gaga, the old witch doctor who lived in the black forest. She was a small, hunchbacked woman with greasy, stringy hair and only two black teeth she used for chewing and spitting bitter tobacco. She came with a white, lit candle in one hand and a pencil holding what little hair she had in a bun. She rolled her eyes at the father when he explained how his daughter was not attracting a man and used the candle to look up the girl's nostrils.

My, said Yadda Gaga, what a tasty little girl you'd have if she wasn't so sour.

Then she pulled out the pencil and poked the girl's arm with the eraser. Where her skin was touched it broke apart and bled. Yadda Gaga spat on the floor.

Take the lemons away, Yadda Gaga said. You can see the sick. Once they're away her skin will toughen up.

She wafted her hand over the girls' hair and retched. Then she let the father look up the girl's nostrils with the white candle, but all he could see was pink skin and hair.

But the daughter cried and said, Oh no, Daddy, don't take your lemons away! I think they are helping me. I might be worse without them.

Her father stared at the black cud on the floor and said, Lemons are my life. Haven't you tasted my lemonade? I've won blue ribbons.

Piss water, said Yadda Gaga and took her leave but not before spitting on the front door.

When she was gone the daughter took her father's hand in her own and said, Daddy, your lemonade is my favorite. Then she said, Ow, when her father squeezed her hand in thanks, and when he looked down his palm was covered in blood.

Because his daughter wept and thrashed and spilled lemon bathwater on the ground when he tried to take them away, he called in the local array of doctors, all of whom had degrees. They were all tall, thin men with moustaches and they towered over the father and his bathing offspring. When they saw the girl they sneered and put clothespins over their noses.

She smells like rotting disinfectant, they said. We smell that quite enough, thank you.

They prodded her arms and legs and took blood in small clear vials and put tubes down her throat, long ones, the kind that made her choke. The felt her breasts for lumps and looked inside her with a shiny new speculum. The father protested, Are you sure it's necessary? but they assured him it was.

Two weeks later they mailed him the results: She needs a man. Get her one. Now. Young girls her age should be in love. See page eighty-seven of *Overcoming Ophelia* for proof. That'll fix her right up. It'll toughen her thin skin if he breaks her heart. It'll toughen her skin if he loves her back. All the other young ladies will be jealous. Jealous young ladies bite.

Also, here's the bill.

p.s. Take care of the bill ASAP.

p.p.s. If that doesn't work try aspirin.

The father wrung his hands and covered his face and said, Oh, where can I find a young man who will love the easily bruised fruit of my loins? He sat on the edge of her bath and asked what sort of man she could easily love the best: Brunette or blond? Tall or short? Fat or thin? What was her opinion on facial hair? Should his nose be aquiline? And what eye color would she like? Are brown irises ugly? To each question she gave a small shrug and said whatever he thought was best certainly was best.

I am off to find you a strapping young boyfriend, her father said. But before I go, can I do anything for you?

Just leave me a bucket of the best lemons, please, she said. I wouldn't ask you, only....

She raised her arms out of the water. She had no more fingers, just small stumps, like she had been born without.

Her father wept and kissed her stumps and asked what had happened but she said she did not know, only she thought more lemons might help. So he brought her three bushel baskets of lemons and cursed his luck—marrying away a daughter without fingers would probably be very hard. Then, before he left, he laid out three aspirins and a glass of lemonade on the porcelain edge of the bath.

When he left his doorway he saw Yadda Gaga standing among his lemons, smoking a large pipe and sniffing one of his fruits that had been left unattended on the tree, pale yellow and white with rot. When he approached her, she asked, is your daughter still whole, or does she look like this? Then she curled her withered fingers around the fruit until its insides easily spilled out.

The father shuddered and said, I thank you for the help you have given me and my daughter. If I pay you, will you go away? But Yadda Gaga only said, All bills are eventually paid, have no fear.

The father walked past the edges of his village—none of those boys had wanted his daughter anyhow—and went into the great pastures to find a simple boy who did not care if his girlfriend was whole or not. He talked to every shepherd he came across but they were only interested in women who knew every detail of a sheep's hoof, from the keratin content to guessing its exact diameter from a glance. What use, they asked, was a woman who only cared for lemons? It seemed very narrow minded to them.

He wrote his daughter a letter asking her how she was and if she had her heart set on a shepherd, and she wrote back saying, I suppose. OK. Daddy, my feet have gone. I had to pick five hundred and seven lemons on my knees with my teeth. That old witch stood in the orchard and watched me the entire time. Why won't she go away? I'm writing this letter with the pen between my molars. Won't you come home soon?

So, with little time left to find a man, he went to the stables and approached each stable hand, but they too were only interested in women who knew about horses, or at least could do useful things, like braiding a horse's long tail or tying bows into their manes before shows. The father shook his head and clenched his hand and cursed her missing fingers, for certainly she could have learned how to braid. Even he knew how to do that.

He wrote and asked if she had her heart set on a stable hand, thinking he could glue some twigs to her stumps and she could manage that way. He received a letter that did not say anything at all, but inside was a crushed lemon peel and citrus tears.

Immediately he returned home. He had only been gone a week, but there were two letters from the doctors about the bill in his mailbox, one polite, the other not so.

He walked into his house with his heavy head sagging on his chest. He called out his daughter's name and her reply was so faint and tremulous that he took the stairs three at a time. But in his bathroom he did not see his daughter, only lemon bathwater with two yellow peels floating next to one another, and Yadda Gaga sitting in a chair with her feet propped up on the edge of the tub, smoking her heavy pipe. He called his daughter's name again and asked what the old hag did to his little girl. Yadda Gaga spit and rolled her eyes.

You let her marinate too long, said Yadda Gaga, tapping the edge of her pipe with a crooked finger. She pointed to the lemon peels and said, There, there is your little girl.

The father realized that those were not lemon peels floating in the water, but two bright yellow thick and bumpy human lips. They gathered together in the water and he watched them say, Sorry, Daddy. Five hundred and seven lemons, Daddy. I need five hundred and seven lemons.

Yadda Gaga reached down and plucked the lemon lips from the sour water and placed them between her withered gums and black teeth. She chewed, once, and the father watched his daughter slide down the old throat.

Mermaid

Why should you want to escape us, your sisters who love you more than you know? Why should you want to twist your torso and your long, shimmering scales and dash away, making ripples in your wake? Away. Away. You want to be on their land. You want to breathe their harsh air, hear the screech of their voices, like electric eels in your ear. It burns, sister. How does it not burn you as well?

We have felt your beloved dry sand against our fins, inside the curves of our long fingers. Do you know how it rips our delicate bodies, softened by a lifetime saturated in water and salt? You will rip apart like anemone in the storm. We will find your new body, transformed from the quick, slick fish scales into the ugly feet of a man, lying on that rough sand, the water grazing your still knees. We will not be able to pull you back to us.

Recall when we were young, just after our eyes opened, and we went to the surface and saw the thick, blue body of the mother whale on their beach? Do you remember her tail making its feeble rise—so different from the powerful strokes its muscle could thunder—before it fell into our water and splashed our eyes? We thought it was the sea, but you were making your own salt. You made salt for so long after that day, and we could not comfort you. This is what you want, sister, this air that makes our kind weak?

All this suffering for a man you barely know.

You look so much like us, he does not know it is not your dark hair floating on the surface like a corpse, does not know it is not your lips reaching toward his, not your hands digging into his shoulders. It is for you we do this. We are made of the same stuff, sister. Your passion was born at the moment of our spawning, and we carry, each of us, a little bit of it inside.

He sighs and parts his arid lips and sinks below our water. We wrap ourselves around him and make a home of our bodies. We are not unkind. You may visit his bones, preserved forever between us, drifting in our waves, a little forgotten thing in our kingdom below the sea.

Bloody Mary

alter first saw her at the school library, after hours. The new girl. Small-town folk like Salter could always tell when there was something fresh brought in, like ripe apples. She was a mousy girl with big brown hair and bright eyes. She looked lost but cheerful for being so. Attractive, but young, perhaps too young. Salter gave her one last up and down and slid into the stacks, walking the familiar route. Not too many students went through the library; there were few books anyway, and the ones they did have were so old they had as much dust on their covers as they were filled with words. They knew that the back stacks were a forbidden place, not legally, but their parents would slap their faces if they brought home one of those books, the ones with monsters on the covers, the ones about the old forests and their ancient residents. The ones the library had to carry, because it was a library, but no one approved of.

Salter chose the book because its spine was uncracked. There was something special about a book that had never been opened except, of course, for the removal of its dust jacket, which Salter considered a kind of stripping, an honest laying bare of the insides. She was honored to be the first to touch it, to really look inside.

The folklore section was small, populated with texts with frightening titles like *The Dangers of the Occult* and *The Devil Inside*. If Daddy caught her, she'd have to recite passages of the Bible until her throat was raw, as if the memorization of those words could erase what she had seen.

The new girl followed her, maybe intentionally, maybe by accident, but she was there, staring at her with an open curiosity, not unkind, but the sort of earnestness that was born from loneliness. Salter sneered at the girl until she lowered her eyes and walked off. Salter peered around the stacks to make sure no one was looking. She put the book in her bag and looked around again.

"Find anything interesting?" the librarian asked when Salter dutifully rooted around her pockets for her library card.

"Just this," she said, tapping on the cover of a thick book she had grabbed randomly off the shelf. *The Lives of the Saints.*

"Heavy reading for a young girl."

"My dad said it was a good one."

"He's right."

* * *

There was an oft-told joke among the girls that Indiana was known as the crossroads state because there was not anything worth stopping for. One only traveled its roads to get somewhere better, like Chicago or Cincinnati or, if they had enough gas, all the way to New York City. There was a magic to those places, and they would whisper the names of those cities before they went to bed each night, hoping to wake up there. They were disappointed to always wake up in Madison, Indiana, a city that was not a city, not as they understood a city, in a state that was hardly a state. Yet they made the best of living in a space where there was, as far as they were concerned, very little living to do beyond loitering outside of the gas station while Morrow promised undelivered blowjobs for loosies to the pimple-faced attendant. If there was no living to do where they were born, they would make the best of what they were given. On days when the weather was clear, they linked arms and walked South to Utica, a place as miserable and cold as where they had been born, but for one special place rooted in the woods.

Later, they learned that it was called the Witches Castle, a place where those with pure hearts had burned nine women to death and sang and danced and pissed on their ashes. A stone building, covered in graffiti and moss, a place that the witch from the story their parents told them when they were but tiny little things would have appreciated, once she gave up that candy-child-killer thing. The girls brought folding chairs and blankets and pillows and small mirrors so they could practice putting on the makeup they were disallowed at school, except for ChapStick, which they always slathered on to make their lips shine.

There was a ceremony to their arrival. They would dump their bags and share equally the spoils of what they had taken: sandwiches from home, the cheap, bright red lipstick from the store they'd pocketed when the attendant was looking the other way, eggs from farms and flowers from fields, cigars and, when they were particularly lucky, father's throat-searing gin. Almond, all wicked grins and rolled eyes, had a habit of stealing hunting knives from her brothers, and these she laid out reverently in a small row from smallest to largest. She sharpened them on the edges of the door and would run them up and down her legs to slice off the fine hairs that had begun to grow three years ago and which she was continuously disgusted by. Morrow passed out the loosies and bellowed with laughter when she recounted how hopeful the attendant had looked, standing outside in the alley, waiting for her to pucker her lips around him.

"Fucker'll be waiting a long time," she told them, running her hand through her short hair. The girls laughed with her.

"You'll have to pay up eventually. He'll catch on," Almond said.

Helene, the beautiful, shiny-haired, thick-lipped one, brought candles and a lighter (*Fuck, fancy,* they'd said in admiration) and a waggle to her eyebrows. "They never catch on. Tell him your mother saw you and made you go home. Cry a little. He'll think you're in love."

"Gross," Morrow said.

Salter always shared last. She, better than any of them, had a sense of the theatrical and knew patience. She upended her bag once they had turned their attention to eye shadow.

"You brought a book?" Almond said, scrunching her nose. "School's over today."

"Fuck you," Salter said. "Just because you can't read doesn't mean the rest of us are bores."

"What is it?" asked Helene, turning it over so she could see the cover. She whistled low.

"I can read," Almond said.

Salter grabbed the book and held it up to the girls. "See this," she said, tapping the cover, "those who came before us."

They peered with a reverence Salter felt appropriate. Helene reached out a trembling hand and caressed the cover. Together, they opened it, and Morrow read aloud, "The Lives of Witches."

"History," Almond moaned, falling onto her back and sprawling her hands. "That's boring."

"Shut your mouth," Salter said. "They've got a bit here on the Bloody one."

Almond sat up and reached for another loosie. "Go on, then," she said.

Salter told them how girls in the days of frilly skirts and long night-gowns used to play all sorts of games with one another to tell the future. They'd wait until it was pitch dark and light a candle. Then, in their nightclothes, they would walk up their stairs backwards without pause or fear, because you had to walk evenly for the game to work.

"That's how they all died," Morrow said. "Tripped over their own feet."

When they reached the top of the stairs, they could then turn around and walk into their bedrooms. With a floor-length mirror, and it had to be floor-length so they could see their whole bodies, they would hold their candles to their faces and whisper her name three times: Bloody, Bloody, Bloody. If they were lucky, if they did the chant right and Bloody was awake, she would appear to them as a young and beautiful woman and show them the face of the one they were meant to marry: those kind faces of boys who would treat them right and let them spend money on new dresses for Sunday, and who would spring for steak once a month if the factory was producing. But if Bloody was in a bad mood, or thought the girl was not taking it as seriously as she should take prophesy, they'd see her in her moment before her death with her skin stripped off her bone and empty holes for eyes. She'd open her mouth and show you exactly what happened to you after you died, the whole of emptiness down her throat, and you'd go bleak, stark mad.

Helene smiled and puckered her lips at Salter.

"You two are gross," Almond said, dodging the lipstick Salter threw at her.

"We should try it," Morrow said. "Summon her, or whatever."

"We'd have to prepare," Helene said. "Do it right."

Salter, all-knowing as she had read the passages an hour ago, told them they'd need to find a sacrifice to give to the Bloody Mother. All the girls who saw death messed it up because they hadn't offered anything in return.

"All we got are mosquitos," Almond said, flicking one off of her ankle.

When they left, each of them began the process of hiding their stash, pulling up the floorboards and burying the good stuff: lipsticks and blush and eye shadow and knives and half-full handles of liquor. They wrapped the pillows in their blankets and covered those with crunched leaves. They redrew a line of chalk at the door and windows to keep out the ants. They blew out their candles and buried them.

Salter hooked her arm with Helene. "Saw new meat at the library. Young thing."

"Saw her first," Helene said. "Moved in next to me. El Ay girl. Her name is Mary. Cute."

Salter roiled her stomach until it cramped against the cold chicken salad she'd swiped from the supermarket and scarfed for lunch hours ago. "But not as cute as me, yeah?"

"No one's as cute as you."

* * *

As a child, Salter learned to associate the word Daddy with the following: fat, fuck, fight. Daddy-Fat. Daddy-Fuck. Daddy-Fight. Though the family had an extra bedroom in their little house, he placed boxes from floor to ceiling, which he had whimsically called his paperwork. Salter was forced to sleep in the large bed with him and her mother, because mattresses were expensive and it was even more expensive to heat a whole other room, and anyway, he gargled at her, the family who sleeps together stays together. There was always a burlesque performance before bed, the way he would peel his dirty clothes away from his dirty body and place them atop an ever growing pile in the corner of the room, which only diminished when her mother saved up enough coins to haul them to the pay laundry. Then he would watch Salter and her mother undress, before Salter caught onto his game and made a point to use the bathroom half an hour before and slip under the covers, closing her eyes and practicing breathing evenly. No matter how hard she willed it, she could not evenly breathe away his body next to hers, the unbearable heat of his flesh, and the cold, small body of her mother, who always kept her face to the wall, as close to the edge as she could be without falling off. Salter had to make her body small between them, sweating and freezing, the dark stink of Daddy's breath shifting her hair. Above her, the half-naked and beaten body of the Christ hung loose, a small rivulet of red paint dribbling out from his side. It was a long time before she learned to sleep under him, always imagining that blood would fall as soon as she closed her eyes and he would drown her.

Once, when Daddy was at work, she looked into his boxes of paperwork and found rocks. She stayed up all night and clenched her fingers, wondering if she was strong enough to strangle him.

* * *

Every morning, Salter followed the same procedure before she went to school. Her daddy, perpetual over-sleeper, would have to be bypassed as quietly as possible. Rolling out of the bed, she had long learned how to dim the lights enough to see what she was going to wear that day, and how slowly to open the closet so that it didn't squeak. She'd grab handfuls of clothes and change in the bathroom, then slip back into the bedroom and exchange the book in her bag for the hidden one in the back of the closet. No foul if daddy found it while she was at school. He might accuse her of being unclean, but he couldn't object to her reading choice.

* * *

Math was her most difficult subject, but Salter appreciated numbers, even if they made no sense to her. She liked that she could divide and multiply them together in strings a hundred long and still come to something nice and neat by the end calculation. Her teacher, unshaven and paunch-bellied, was her favorite because he paid the least attention to her.

"Class," he said, "we have a new student, all the way from Los Angeles."

Salter looked up and saw the girl from the library, seemingly embarrassed, red-cheeked, staring at the floor. She felt a momentary smidge of sympathy for the girl, having to stand in front of all of them like a new show dog.

"This is Mary Hallowell. What brings you to our small corner of the world, Mary?"

"My dad got a new job? At the glass factory?" Mary said.

"Seems a long way to travel just to work the floor. Economy must be bad everywhere." Her teacher said, frowning. "No positions out West?"

"No? He's a lawyer."

Mary's new shoes spoke the truth of what it meant to have a lawyer for a father: a man who so loved his baby girl that he bought her white shoes and knew she wouldn't ruin them, who gave her a backpack that had only recently had a price tag on it, not something discovered with dust in the back of a church rummage sale, who may have even paid to have her hair permed, not some botched job done at home with the money carefully collected off the streets and saved in a glass jar in the corner of a closet.

"Welcome, all the same. Now, I like to have my students seated alphabetically, so let's move everyone down a bit. Come on now, on your feet, stop that bellyaching. Moving helps your brain focus. Mary, take your seat over here."

Mary sat next to Helene. Helene wiggled her fingers and smacked her gum.

"Hey, neighbor. Got a pencil I can borrow?" Helene whispered.

Mary dug into her backpack and handed her a number two, unsharpened, yellow, and free of teeth marks. Their fingers brushed and lingered in the exchange. Helene twisted her long hair into a bun and jammed the pencil in the middle to hold. "Thanks, doll."

Salter scratched in the edges of her book. *Bitch.*

* * *

Lunch was the only time when the girls could gather without being watched by the adults, where they did not need to be accounted for in a seat. They met at different places each day, palming notes to one another in the hallways with the number of an unused classroom, or outside in the alley between the school and a few rundown homes where the kids who wore black sold overpriced loosies and weed. Morrow was on the rag, and she did not suffer bleeding alone, so her note demanded that they meet in a far, cramped bathroom away from the cafeteria.

"Fucking hell," she said, slamming her fist on the side of the tampon dispenser on the wall. "It ate my nickel!"

Salter sat on a dry sink and dug around in her pockets. "If I had one I'd give it to you. Just make a plug." She gestured toward the cheap toilet paper in the open stall.

"Want me to send some under?" Almond said from the occupied stall.

Morrow groaned. "Too scratchy. Maybe I'll fake butt cancer and go home for the day."

Salter shrugged and put a half-used roll in her bag. Occasionally her mother forgot to replace the empties at home, and so she had taken to stashing emergency supplies under the sink, behind the cleaning supplies that must have been purchased on a whim, because they had never been used.

Helene poked her head in the door. "This the right place? I can barely read Morrow's scratch."

"Obviously," Salter said, grinning.

She walked in, scrunching her long brown hair with one hand as she did. After her trailed a mousy, nervous looking girl, holding her purse strap in front of her with both hands. Salter felt sick for a brief moment, and wondered if she too might be getting her period.

"Everyone," Helene said, "This is the new girl, Mary."

Morrow slammed her hand against the dispenser again. "Hey."

"You're in my biology class!" said Almond, followed by a low splash. "Ugh, finally."

Salter almost told Mary to get the fuck out, but Helene skipped over and placed a kiss on her cheek. Salter smiled, even though she was still angry, and didn't quite know why she felt that way.

"Either of you got a dime?" Morrow asked.

Helene shook her head. Mary dug around in her purse, her hand trembling. "I have a dollar?" she held it up.

"Machine only takes coins," Morrow said, but she snatched the dollar and folded it into her pocket.

Mary glanced back and forth between all the girls, and Salter wondered exactly how young she was. Maybe she was one of those smarty-pants girls who skipped a few grades when she was a kid because her parents were pushy folk who believed the sun rose and set each day in blessing that they had managed to fuck and get a baby out of it. She'd known a boy like that before he transferred to a private school. Always raised his hand, even when the teacher didn't ask for answers. Always asked more questions than anyone cared to know about the subject. She'd pushed him against the lockers once and stared at him until he lowered his eyes, and he was smart enough to know what she meant. He stopped raising his hand in classes with her.

"God dammit," Morrow said, punching the dispenser.

"What's wrong?" Mary asked, then seemed surprised that she had said anything, and shifted her weight back and forth. "Is it stuck? Let me try something."

Mary handed Helene her purse and bent under the dispenser, peering up. She stuck her hand up the machine, scrunched her face, hit the side of it. She took a deep breath, closed her eyes, and then pulled her hand out, holding two tampons.

"Well, fuck me sideways. You're handy. Literally." Morrow snatched a tampon and went into the other stall.

"What happened?" Almond asked.

"I have small hands," Mary said. "At my old school, the machine jammed all the time. Anyone want the extra?"

Salter snatched it when she saw Helene making a move. "Thanks," she said.

Helene was practically preening. "Ain't she cool? Her parents still have a place in California. Mary said if they go out there I might go with them. Maybe I'll see a real movie star. Wonder if they're so shiny in real life."

* * *

Salter clutched the tampon in her fist the rest of the school day, almost snapping it in half when Helene gave her a quick lip-kiss, saying that Mary's parents were picking her and Mary up and taking them to dinner. Mary extended an invitation to Salter, saying there was more than enough room in her parents' minivan, but Salter shrugged her off with an excuse that her parents were expecting her. In truth, she had no desire for Mary and her clean shoes to see Daddy's overgrown lawn and the paint-chipped sidings, the gutters choked with leaves, or his fat-fuck body sitting on the porch, as he sometimes did, his belly hanging out, swigging from a flask and reading the Bible.

Her mother was home when Salter arrived, which meant she either did not go to work or she left early. Her father dozed on the couch while her mother stirred a pot of boiling water, upturning pasta into it. Ketchup and butter noodles and hot dogs. When she was younger, sometimes her mother would cut the hot dogs into octopuses, or arrange them in a smiley face over the noodles, but she had not done that in years. Now, her mother dropped the dog on top, when they had dogs.

Without saying hello, Salter kneeled in the closet in the bedroom, replacing the *Lives of the Witches* with *The Lives of the Saints*, the latter she hid behind her father's muddied work shoes in case her father rifled through her bag. She went outside and sat on the back porch and tossed the tampon from one hand to the other, amazed at herself for hating such a small, meaningless thing.

Maybe Helene and Mary were eating steak together, and mashed potatoes and something green. Helene was endlessly charming, and she could talk to whomever she wanted and make them feel like she understood them, that they were special. When Salter first met Helene, she tried to imitate her, tried to walk like her and make the same eye contact and smile, but people didn't react to her the way they did Helene. Instead, when she smiled and stared, her mouth would hurt and her eyes would water, not knowing when to look away or blink, and people reacted suspiciously, asking her what she had done, responding in halting sentences, not answering her questions until she just dropped the act and stopped making the attempt. But Helene never stopped talking to her, said she liked her dirty clothes, liked the way her skin tasted, like salt and dirt and all sorts of real earthy things. What if Helene tasted Mary and liked how she tasted better? Mary, who probably tasted like expensive soaps and some kind of fruit, sweet and airy. Impossible, expensive things.

Salter pulled a lighter out of her back pocket and flicked it on. She lit the end of the tampon and watched it smolder then catch and fire up. The plastic and cotton burned and smelled awful, but Salter breathed it all in. She thought of all those women who were burned to death by angry mobs who didn't understand them, who thought they were evil, and maybe they were evil and deserved what they got, but who really could say. At the end, they may have cried out for some dark force to save them, to make them greater than they were and burn those who would burn them.

"Dinner," her mother said listlessly from the porch. Salter stamped the tampon out, covered it with dirt, and went inside.

* * *

Morning, Daddy awake and staring at her. At first, she thought he was just so drunk he forgot to close his eyes, but dark little pupils followed her around the room while she fisted underwear, a shirt, and a bra. He smiled at her, a great big grin, and she saw the black where his teeth met his gums, like dirty glue holding everything together. Salter stared back, waiting for him to lower his eyes, praying the Bloody Mother would rip them out and eat them, but he matched her eye for eye. If she waited longer with him, she would miss the bus and have to walk, and if she was late for class there would be a telephone call home, and that would give the fat fuck an excuse, so she clenched her fingers around her clothes, grabbed a pair of jeans, and went into the bathroom. She heard him laughing, even as she walked out the door.

* * *

The girls met at the Witches Castle and spilled their goods: Morrow's loosies, the crayons Helene snatched from the art room, and a hair tie Almond un-wove from her hair and dropped on the pile.

"Slow day," she said defensively, when the girls looked at her.

Salter sat her backpack on the ground and went to her knees next to Helene. "Have a good time with the new thing?" she asked.

Helene raised her arms above her head and fell onto Salter. "Jealous," she said affectionately, trying to poke Salter on the nose. "Aw, come on, she's not so bad." Helene reached for two cigarettes, lit them, and placed one between Salter's lips. "Where's your contribution?"

Salter wished she hadn't buried that tampon, wished she'd stuck it in her bag and brought it with her to put on the pile. She could call it art or any such thing, and then Helene would know what she felt, all that ugly inside of her, and she wouldn't have to try to put it into words. Instead, she grunted that she had brought the book. She upended her backpack and ignored the laughter of the others when *The Lives of the Saints* fell out. Salter swore loudly.

It was easy enough to convince them to do the ritual of the Bloody Mother, mostly because they had no idea what it might entail, and neither did she. Every book she had read on the subject had been frustratingly vague in its description, only mentioning that the women had done spells and tricks and rituals, but absolutely no detail was given, except slim descriptions that may have included dancing or sacrificing a small animal, but no indication if, it was dancing, how their feet ought to move and, if it was sacrifice, what sort of knife to use and where to cut.

"We've got plenty of knives," Morrow said, indicating Almond's neat pile of sharp blades, her shirt riding up to her shoulder as she lifted her arm. A large hand of bruised fingertips at the top of her pale arm, brown and blue and yellowed at the edges, roughed and marring her skin. The girls all noticed, and Morrow matched their stares. They said nothing to one another, did not have to, for each of them had, at one point, brought bruises or scars on their bodies into the Witches Castle, and they knew better than to voice it aloud. It was their place of power, and any indication that they might be weak was to be taken off when they entered and put back on when they left. Inside, they could pretend, and it was glorious to pretend. Helene pushed extra cigarettes over to Morrow, and that was all that had to be done.

As the sun fell, Helene passed out mirrors to the four of them, compacts that had been swiped from mothers or from counters at the mall. They wiped off the paint from their faces, and Almond and Morrow made off first while the other two girls lagged behind.

"Tell me something good," Salter asked Helene, grabbing the girl's hand and entwining it with her own in her pocket.

Helene hummed, then told her about how one day their parents were going to die, as all parents must, and they would leave behind their houses. The two of them would live in the house, alone, together. They would dig up the ground in the yard until they hit the hidden water in the soil. Frogs would move there, and try to kiss them with their slimy lips. The two of them would pluck a frog and bring it to their faces, stick out their tongues, and whack them into walls. Each night, they would dine on frog legs. And it would be good until they too passed, and then the wood would grow around them and bury them inside, wrapped up around one another. Helene, more than the rest of them, had goodness inside of her, and could express it in a manner the other girls had lost, or a skill they had never been born with. Salter took comfort in that goodness, though she never voiced how afraid she was that it might all be only wishes.

* * *

Salter lived in a home of edges and sharp air. Daddy sat at the kitchen table, flipping pages in her thick library book. This, she knew, was a confrontation waiting release, and she reminded herself that she could not control him or what he would do, but said a prayer to the Bloody Mothers before her that she might walk away from it with little hurt this time.

"Interesting stuff," Daddy said pleasantly. He smiled widely at her, and she focused on his rotting gums, hoping whatever sickness grew there festered to his heart. "This required reading at your school?"

She knew no answer would appease him, so she stared. When she was a child, when he was drinking and the alcohol made him bloodshot and wild and he would hit her, any noise of protest she made gave him pleasure. But her silence unnerved him, made him grasp for something to say. It also made him return to her, open hand whacking her face, over and over again through the hours of his rage, but she never squealed until she wanted it to end. It was worth the bruises, that small amount of unease she could cause.

He stood. "Underlining in your library books is a serious offense, girl. They charge you for that. Think we got money?" He handed her the book and pointed to a passage she'd starred in the margins. "Read that."

Salter swallowed. "I need water. Throat's dry."

He filled a glass with water and gave her a sip before taking it back. "Don't spill on the book. Now, read."

"Depending on the version, Bloody Mary might be benevolent or malevolent, though in all versions she is an oracle of the future. Victorian women, obsessed with games of divination, chanted her name in a mirror to see the face of their future husband. It was there that, if the woman were to die before she married, she would see death's head. Modern variations of her story indicate that her legend has soured. When she appears recently, she shows the penitent their deaths, and then leads them towards it. In all variations, she is covered in blood, indicating her own miserable fate."

His paunch gut brushed up against her side, and she thought about those thick white lines that ran up and down his skin under his shirt, the ones that expanded like worms to his ever-increasing neck.

"We've all got miserable fates, girl."

She saw his fist coming, and because she hated him, she did not close her eyes until he connected with her.

* * *

Salter awoke on an unfamiliar bed, her head heavy as brick, made worse by vulgar male voices laughing. She opened her eyes in stages, trying to get used to the light.

"Sleeping beauty graces us with her presence." That was Daddy. He laughed at his own joke.

"Come now, John. This is a solemn event." It took her a moment to place the other man. Harold Birch III, an old man from Daddy's congregation who smelled like smoke and sugarcane. As soon as her memory placed him she felt the stench of him and groaned to hold in the bile.

"You're right. Forgive me. Nerves, you know? You try to be a good father, and do what's best for your kids. But they run wild, Harry. I can't always be watching."

Harold grumbled low in approval. "You're not alone. Do you know how many parents say the same thing to me? You raise them up right but they turn left. Come, bow your head. Think about your sins, where you led your daughter astray. You read the good book to her, but it is not enough to read. You can't put the Word on her tongue alone, but you must make sure it is in her heart, in her blood, or else she is left bare to corruption. She is young, and a girl. The devil desires them most of all because they are so willing, that is, unless we teach the path."

Salter lifted her head. They were in a cheap motel room. She fingered the cigarette burns on the bedspread and saw cobwebs in the corner. In front of her was a large mirror facing the bed, and she almost screamed when she saw her face, half covered in bandages, red puffed skin at the edges.

Survive this, she told herself. Survive and you can do anything.

"Water, please" she whispered, afraid at the unfamiliar scratch in her tone.

Harold, his clean black suit, his bald head with the sick spots littering his skull and face, smiled at her, kindly, but all she could focus on were his teeth, unnaturally white for a man who smelled as he did. "My dear, our Lord went forty days and forty nights without a single drop in the desert. Can you not go a few hours in his grace?"

"Please," she said again.

Daddy put his head in his hands. "See how she is?"

Harold patted Daddy on the shoulder. "Come now. You must be strong for your daughter. If your faith is weak, then you open up yourself."

Harold handed Daddy a thick black book. He dug into his pocket and brought out a yellowed handkerchief. He wiped his forehead. "Let's begin."

The two men raised their hands over her body and began to read in unison.

* * *

They denied her water each time she asked, and as the hours drew forward she slipped in and out of consciousness, dreaming each time of drowning and being happy for such an end, and each time awoke to their raised voices and raised hands, burning when they lowered their hands to her feet and her head and her hips. No devil in my hips, she wanted to say, but there was not enough saliva to form the words. They sprinkled water on her in intervals, but though she left her mouth wide, none of it landed on her tongue. She tried to think of Helene, of all the goodness that Helene would talk about, tried to clasp onto the memory of her dreams, but the voices of the men interrupted her thoughts, pulled her back into their reality. The hours slithered.

* * *

She tried to speak, to tell them to stop, she would swear anything they wanted if only they would stop. They sat her up when she was unconscious too long and shook her head between their hands until she kept her eyes open. There was a mirror directly in front of her, and saw the bandage on the left side of her face, white around the edges and pink near the middle. The men moved their mouths and hands again, but they moved a rusted bucket to the foot of the bed. They held up the book of the mothers, of her witch ancestors, and they slathered top to bottom and side to side in oil. They made her watch as they lit a match near the side and dropped it in. It blazed up, blazed bright, and she felt the heat gnash against her body. Her own head floating above the flames.

She moved her lips to form salvation: *Bloody Mother, Bloody Mother, Bloody Mother,* for if ever there was a time of sacrifice and need, this was it. The movement cracked lips, but the sting kept her awake. And then, she saw herself change. The bandages on her face darkened from white to pink and then red goo, dripping downward across her face and then her body. It moved upward, sleeking through her hair, hot yet cool, a comfort. Blood. She knew a gift when she saw one, and almost laughed with the joy of being so beloved by her protector, the sublime fervor of knowing that all you believed was real. The blood coagulated and spun, red swirls, and then trailed itself into her nose and eyes. She tasted the cool iron and was sated. Her own eyes darkened before her until they were like nothing at all, containing nothing, and ever expanding outward in a flush of red. The blood is the life, all blood is life, and in herself she felt the power of the Bloody Mother.

Once, Salter had told Helene that the four of them had been born angry, and weaseled out from between their mother's legs in full rage. It was not unusual, she'd said, as all girls are born that way, knowing from the moment they hit the outside air that they were in for a heavy dose of unfairness and pain. Most girls, though, their anger was tempered down by pretty things and kind parents and the need to hide it, because angry girls were beat up and beat down until they were made soft, like dough. Helene had laughed at her, kissed her brow and said she wasn't angry, but Salter put her hand on the girl's chest and felt the splutter of her heart, diminished rage, the kind that matched her own. And they'd slipped off their clothes and bit one another and intermingled their hands and legs, and Helene had admitted that yes, there was much to be angry about, but it was safer, wasn't it, to be calm, to pretend at peace.

When the bald man and Daddy lowered their hands onto her body, and Daddy's fingers inched towards her breast, she felt the familiar comfort of hate swell up in her, and she knew the Bloody Mother would accept nothing less than her at her most honest.

And so, she laughed. She laughed at these men and their Book and their God and all their false things, because the real was in her and it was everything and always and everywhere and…and…

Daddy dumped a cup of water over her head.

* * *

When hurt, the body desires a place of familiar comfort, and in this regard Salter had a body like any other. Keeping to dark roads and high grass, she crept her way into the nice part of town, where the girls with fathers who worked with their heads and not their hands called home. The well-lit, green part of town. She could not avoid the glares of the streetlamps, illuminating, making her bare in their light. Helene lived on the edges of this place, the strange divide between those with and those without. Her father, a mechanic who could smooth-talk, was promoted to manager at his shop, and her mother insisted on moving as close as they could to the pretty houses. For safety, of course, and because it was much nicer to wake up to clean than cracked.

Salter jumped the fence and almost fell on her way over, but she crept to the back end of the ranch house, the draped window of Helene's room, light creeping out on the edges. Salter rapped her hand on the window quiet as she could, and soon Helene peered half her head around, then opened the window.

"What happened to you?" Helene asked, partial awe and partial horror coloring her words.

Salter climbed into the room and into Helene's arms, and they knelt with one another, leaning against the bed. Helene stroked her hair and whispered coos and sympathy while Salter grit out the whole thing, detailing in the precise the feel of Daddy's hands on her, and the low wretched sound of the bald man's voice, the hours lost. She told of their eyes, their burning eyes, and how it seemed like she was nude before them, and how much they liked that. Helene rubbed the back of Salter's head, and she cried too. Good things were like that, Salter thought, they cry even when they see shit things get sad.

"I saw her," Salter said.

"Who did you see?"

"The Bloody Mother. She came to me. Helped me. I saw her."

Helene's hand stopped moving on her back, then slowly resumed. "I'm sorry that happened to you," she said.

"Why would you be sorry about that?"

"What your father did."

Salter grasped Helene's hands and held them up to her cheeks. She kissed the knuckles, then the palm. "It don't matter what he did. I've got you. And I've got the Bloody Mother."

"Do you want me to tell you something good?"

"Yes." Salter, desperate. "Yes."

Helene pursed her lips to speak goodness, but the door to her room opened, and there stood Mary in a tank top and short-shorts, bedroom clothes, her hair gathered in a messy bun at the top of her head, and a bowl of steaming popcorn settled in the crook of her arm.

"What is she doing here?" Salter asked, pushing herself away from Helene.

"Sorry," said Mary. "I, that is, I didn't know that you ...," she gestured with one hand, then closed her mouth, seemingly having no idea what to say.

"She's just staying the night," Helene said, lingering on *just*, and Salter felt she should read something of importance into that word, but she felt that rage, the same that made her powerful not too long ago in the room with the men, now feel like sickness settling into her belly. She thought she might vomit.

Helene called her name, but Salter was already on her feet, climbing out the window and back into the dark night, remembering the lonely way back.

* * *

She sought out Morrow first, because Morrow would be the easiest to convince and the easiest to find. Morrow stayed out all night, but she loitered the same places, hung around the regular scenes. If not crouching near the dumpster behind the Quick Gas, she'd be walking the strip mall, waiting for an attendant to turn their heads, quick to snatch a small thing, quick to pocket and quick to run.

"The hell happened to you?" Morrow said.

"Dad-fuck."

Morrow nodded. That said enough. The details of pain were unnecessary between them. For Morrow, it was "Bro-fuck", and Salter knew about that boy's wandering hands, lingering too low on a hug, insisting on lip-kisses when greeting, hand in Morrow's short hair. Once, he'd put his dick in her, and she'd told her parents because she didn't know any better, and they'd done the right thing and told him to get out, but within a month they'd let him back in, because he was first born and their only son, and after all, they had three other daughters, and didn't you know how hard it was to be separated from that which you love? The girls had a plan once; Salter was going to get him alone, seduce him and then put her heel down on his balls, but he wouldn't take the bait, and Helene, who could have seduced him, was too afraid of his hands.

"Call Almond. Tell her to meet us."

Morrow pulled out the dollar she'd taken from Mary and went into the Quick Gas to make change. She came out and gave Salter a cigarette, then went to the payphone and dialed.

* * *

Almond was put out. "Are you sure it said we have to sacrifice something?"

The girls sat against the wall of the Witches Castle, foregoing the ritual of sharing goods. Morrow unwrapped the bandage from Salter's face, grimaced, then sealed it back up. "It'll scar," she said.

"You can't get anything if you don't give anything," Salter told her.

"What have we got except lip paint?" Almond asked.

Salter insisted, and though Morrow and Almond protested at first, they were wide-eyed when Salter told them about how she'd felt the Mother pull inside her, like a pregnancy, but like all pregnancies had to be nurtured, else it would rot away and be born without brains or eyes, a dumb wailing thing.

"What are you going to do with what the Bloody Mother gives you?" Almond said. "You have to do something."

Morrow answered before Salter could speak. "I'm going to make it so I was never born."

Almond and Salter looked at one another. "You're going to kill yourself?"

Morrow kicked the ground and rolled her eyes. "No. I could do that right now just fine. But then I'd still have all the memories. Even after I'd be dead I'd have the memories. I don't think those go away even after you die, and everyone would still remember me too. So I'm going to go back in time to when I wasn't anything at all and make that sure I stay that way."

Almond made to protest, but Salter cut her off. She understood the impulse to be nothing and remain nothing, had wished it herself many times when she saw the shit man who had helped in her creation and knew she was stuck with him in some manner because of his blood. She told Morrow that it was something they could do, once the Bloody Mother had blessed them, and she'd even combine her power to help her achieve it.

They went home as normal, the plan simmering beneath their skins. They agreed not to tell Helene, because Helene was, they all agreed, something like beautiful, and there was no reason to get beauty messed up in performance. They would tell her after and, if it worked, they would let her in on the next one, so that she too could be granted the benevolence of the Mother.

* * *

Almond was supposed to be the bait, but she had a gnat for a mother and had inherited that kind of memory, and so Salter ended up knocking on the door of Mary's home. When there was no answer, she knocked again. Shuffling, and then a short woman opened the door and stuck her head out. "Yes?"

"Does Mary live here?"

The woman opened the door wide. "Oh, yes. Are you a friend of hers? Come in."

"She's in my math class," Salter said.

"What happened to your face?"

"I fell."

The house was fancy, but nothing nice enough to get pictured inside of a glossy. The walls had pictures of the family, mother—the woman who opened the door—and a father, a man with a moustache and a smile, and then Mary in various stages of age, from baby to girl with pink shorts and scuffed knees and now, mousy-faced, frizzed hair, beloved, beloved, beloved.

The real Mary bounded down the stairs, pausing briefly when she saw Salter. "Hey," she offered, uncertain, shifting on her feet.

Mary's mother smiled. "You girls want something to drink? Snacks? I can whip up something."

Salter imagined herself as Helene, and wondered what she would say now, the kind of nice thing Helene knew how to do, make everyone feel comfortable in her presence.

"No," Salter said. "I'm watching my weight."

Mary's mother's face fell, and Salter felt the woman's eyes on her legs and arms, the boniness of her, the taut skin on her knees. But the woman muttered something and left.

"I didn't say anything," Mary told her, lowering her voice. "At Helene's? I didn't tell anyone what I saw."

"Don't matter," Salter said. "Look, Helene, she's ... she's my girl-friend, OK?"

"OK," Mary said.

"Do you like her?"

"Sure."

"Are you looking to fuck her?"

Mary stared, and Salter was reminded how young the girl was. "Don't know what I mean? Fuck, you know, put your hands on her thighs, tongue in her mouth, let her do the same to you."

"I don't—"

"Forget it. Look. It's fine if you do. Understandable. It doesn't mean we have to be enemies."

Mary nodded and looked at the floor.

"All of us love her. You can't help it. Just a thing that happens when you're around her. So that makes you one of us, you understand?"

Mary nodded.

"Come on, then."

* * *

Almond talked with Mary on the way over, which suited Salter just fine. The girl was full of wonder and nervousness, making note of everything they passed, even the fast food restaurants. How young this girl was.

When they arrived, Mary was rightfully in awe of the Witches Castle. Her whole body spoke of happiness as she reached out her hand and touched the old stones. She wiped her feet before she entered. Morrow offered her a cigarette, which Mary accepted, puffed without inhaling, and then coughed violently when Almond showed her how to do it properly. They showed her their hidden makeup, and let her put on the reddest lipstick they had. She did it sloppily, obviously new to the whole thing, until they explained it had to be done a certain way, not slathered all over like ChapStick.

The three of them stood around her, watching her feel the stones again, nicking her finger and placing it in her mouth. "Ouch."

"Careful," Morrow said, glancing at the others. "You might hurt yourself."

They fell on her, and at first she did not react, but then she started to shake and cry out, they hit her with their firsts, kicked her in the belly, and Salter stomped her ankle. They used fishing wire cut from Almond's father's rods. The worst part was the screaming. This sort of thing must have been new to Mary, because these girls had all learned that screaming just makes it worse, and it was better to hold that all inside of you until it was over. So they gagged her with a piece of cloth ripped from Morrow's shirt.

When she was trussed up, they sat around her and took the time to breathe deep. Salter snapped open the floorboards and took out the knives, which only made Mary squeal until they kicked her to quiet.

"How we gonna do this without the book?" Morrow asked Salter.

"I know what to say." She hit her palm to her chest. She did it again when Morrow scowled.

The girls followed Salter's instructions and placed their palms against the other, each with a knife between them.

"Holy Mother," Salter began, and Morrow and Almond followed her lead, repeating after her. "Bloody Mother."

"Bloody Mother," they chanted. "Bloody Mother."

They kneeled in front of Mary and began to make shallow cuts on her knees, on her belly, between her toes and on her palms. Salter put her knife up below Mary's eyes and said, "You move, and I will lay you so low the earth won't remember where I've buried your bones."

Mary stilled, and Salter cut two lines on her face so that the tears and blood would mix with the snot. They laughed and flexed their hands, telling one another how they already felt the strength. The Bloody Mother was smiling down on them. When Mary was more wetness than skin, they stopped and put down their knives. They would have to wait until night to finish.

* * *

They took turns watching her while the other two would sit outside and smoke. The day dragged, and they had to beat Mary each time she made a noise, but soon enough she figured out the game and stayed silent. Salter was the one who saw her piss herself, but she said nothing. Each girl expressed, quietly to the other, how surprisingly easy it was to do the things that had been done to them to someone else, almost like the memory had been beaten into their bones and now they could perform the same without much trouble.

Helene arrived when the sun was near the horizon and the sky was red. Morrow kept her outside and called for Salter, who stepped out while the other two girls went in.

"You OK?" Helene asked, putting her hand on Salter's temple. "Ah, he got you. He got you good. But it'll heal. Always does. Why didn't anyone tell me we were coming here?"

Salter put her head on Helene's shoulder and breathed her in.

"Tell me something good," Salter said. "Please."

Helene wrapped her arms around the girl.

"What if your bruises healed? That would be good."

"Not good enough."

Helene rocked Salter back and forth. She started to list all sorts of changes that might be ahead of them, still: cars, the coasts, kicking their cigarette habit, even their skin getting so hard that once someone hit them again they wouldn't even feel it, because they'd be immune.

"Not good enough."

Helene said, "Whatever happens, I'll be there."

"Promise?" Salter said. "Yeah?"

Helene almost promised, but her head turned toward the stone house when she heard a squeal. She detangled her body and went inside, Salter trailing after.

"She won't shut up," Morrow said, slapping the bound girl on the back.

Mary wailed much louder than they'd heard her do before when she saw Helene.

After all this, Salter thought she would take some kind of joy or comfort in Helene seeing the girl like this, but she felt nothing at all, not even as Helene protested, as asked them what the fuck they were doing, as she took a swing at Morrow for standing in her way, but Morrow had long since learned how to duck. Even when Helene started to cry as much as the girl, she didn't feel one thing one way or the other, just a kind of memory that she should probably feel something, but was not quite sure what.

But she did know that she loved Helene, so she told her what they were going to do, how they had to do this dirty thing to summon the Bloody Mother, because they were sick as shit at being beaten down like they were, and so it was their turn. Helene only cried harder, but that was just the sort of good person she was, the kind of girl who would cry for just about anything, because she could feel whatever she wanted to for anyone.

Helene asked why it had to be Mary, of all the people-fucks who they lived around, and all the people-fucks in the entire world.

"Because she isn't us," Salter said.

Helene sniffed, then she nodded, said she understood, in the way they always understood one another. "I can't stay for this," Helene said, running a hand over her swollen, mucky face. She looked Mary straight in the eye as the younger girl started crying hard. "I don't have an excuse, I gotta go back home. They're expecting me. They might come looking."

They walked outside, and Salter fully expected Helene to tell her she was crazy, to demand that she let Mary go and be done with this whole mess, or worse, that none of this was real, and she'd made the whole Bloody Mother thing up, it was just a story in a book full of lies.

Instead, Helene wiped her eyes and asked if Salter wanted to hear one last good thing.

Of course.

"There isn't nothing good left anymore."

* * *

Mary's eyes were closed when Salter came back inside, and Morrow said she had to kick her to keep her quiet, and she may have kicked too hard. Salter did not say so, but she thought that might be a kindness after all.

"Did you bring it?" Salter asked Morrow, who nodded in the affirmative. She went outside and came back with a red gallon jug. Almond wobbled on her feet.

"This isn't funny anymore," she said.

Salter turned to her and bared her teeth. "Are you out?"

"Course not," Almond said. "Just saying. Not funny."

"It isn't supposed to be."

They followed Salter's lead. She cut her own palms and wiped the blood over her face, because they must mirror the Bloody Mother, as she had in the motel. She repeated, Bloody Mother, Bloody Mother, Bloody Mother, and shivered across her whole body. This is how magic must happen, the kind of magic for unlucky girls, their whole bodies twisted up and their voices going numb as they repeated the words. Morrow emptied the jug on Mary, and the sweet stench of the gas made it all the more real what they were about to do. What they were about to become.

Salter lit a cigarette, took a long breath in, and dropped it onto the girl.

The fire was fast, and it consumed far quicker than it ought to have, but that too was just part of the ceremony of the whole thing, and the heat was the magic, and the blood that oozed out was the magic, and though Morrow kept her distance and Almond backed up as far as she could, shaking her head, Salter stepped closer, and waved the flame toward her, breathing in the smoke as she could any burning thing she put in her mouth.

She burned all the things she hated in that girl's body, and then she burned fat-fuck Daddy too, the lazy fuck, and his cramped house and his boxes of rocks, and she burned her mother because she lived in that house without living. The fire spread in a straight line across the whole shit town, and knew it must be erupting up like a beautiful thing, washed pure in flames. She burned the church where the old man lingered, made sure to spend a few extra minutes on his hands and mouth, really tear him up good. She spread it out all around them, from coast to coast, and then jumped across the water, and burned everything on the other side of it all. She burned just outside, because she wanted to burn as well. The Bloody Mother wouldn't let her come to harm, not at the height of her power. This was love, after all, the kind that hurt as much as it made what it cherished powerful, and everything had ever hurt and would ever hurt would be crisped and dead. Once she stepped outside she would walk along the ashes until she found Helene, who was not allowed to burn, because good things could not burn like the rest of the garbage, and together they would dig until they found green things buried under the ash, and start again. There was still worth left, underneath.

She was fire itself.

Morrow was the one who threw water over the dead girl, and the splash hit Salter. She looked outside, fully expecting the charred remains, for how could it be anything less, when it had been so very very hot?

It was as green and dark and clear as it had ever been.

Salter dug up one of their handheld mirrors and looked at her reflection, and what she saw looking back at her was what she always saw, the same nothing face, the reddened skin and acne scars, the same brown eyes, the same unbrushed hair. Only there was her own blood on her cheeks, just as she had left it outside of her body.

"There isn't fucking anything!" Salter, screaming. "There wasn't supposed to be nothing!"

She shook the dead girl's body, willing anything to come out, residual magic that must be there. She screamed and screamed until the night erupted in blue and red lights, and wailing sirens and voices, and she heard men's voices, guttural, telling the girls to put up their hands, and then Helene's voice, crying, telling them to please don't shoot, please do not shoot, those are my friends. Morrow fell to her knees and bit her lips together to keep them shut, but Almond ran, crying out that she didn't know, didn't know, until one of the men in blue tackled her and forced her face into the ground. A man was wrenching her arms behind her and saying something, but all Salter heard was his disgust, the way he couldn't quite form a sentence, gagging as he was on the air. Salter met Helene's eyes, saw her mouthing I'm sorry, I'm sorry, but she had no idea what Helene had to be sorry about.

Yet Helene kept crying in a way that made it seem like she would never stop, and all she would be from then on was a body that only held sadness, and Salter knew she had tapped into a cruel, wrong sort of magic after all, because Helene's sorrow would fall to the earth and take root, as all pain does, and every once in awhile, when it rained, it would rise up and remember, and try to hurt whatever came near it, because that kind of thing knows only one way, and no better than that.

juniper

When my father leaves in the morning, my mother asks me to go outside and find the plant with the fleshy leaves and the pinkish-white flowers. I place my thumb and second finger around the olive green buds and strangle them into a basket. When it is so full that the berries drop over the edge, I run home and give them to Mother. She thanks me with a long kiss on my forehead. She fills a jar with water and salt, so much salt that when I stick my finger in the wet and bring it to my lips I pucker. Mother slaps my hand away and tips the basket into the salt water. Some fall onto the table. Those I pluck and plop into my mouth while Mother tightens the jar lid. She places it on a high shelf next to the ripened fruit with a thousand seeds that my father gave her months ago. The jar skims the side of the fruit and, though the jar is smooth, the bright film holding the juice of the seeds has been waiting to break, and the slight jostle makes one of them burst and bleed.

All white and splotchy-pink, my brother cries in Father's bedroom. Mother chops tomatoes with a heavy knife.

Because my brother is too young to play with me, I go outside and climb the juniper tree my father's great-great-great-grandfather planted when he was a little boy. Once, my father told me that the juniper tree used to grow straight up as all trees do, but junipers grow with all their beauty aching at the top, and ours stretched with so much heavy loveliness that the leaves and branches weigh down its trunk. It is bent in half, like a woman craning her arms over her head and behind her knees, and all its loveliness drags on the dirt.

I climb to the top bend and dangle my feet. My brother cries so loudly I can hear him through the window in my father's bedroom, but he does not cry like a brother should. He sounds like a twittering sparrow, those small brown birds with tiny bones and unremarkable voices, but once you hear them you remember the color of your front door, and the way it whines when you pull it open.

The juniper tree is not far from my father's window, and I watch my mother slam into my father's room. Her dress and hands are stained with tomato pulp. My brother, who is not really my brother, stops his twittering. Young though he is, he knows when Mother is angry, and when she enters my father's bedroom she is always angry.

When I was in my mother's belly, Father had prayed for a boy. Yet when he held me he said I was such a beautiful girl that he cried and almost dropped me in his joy, his hands were shaking with so much happiness, that is what he tells me. After, he went out to find a gift for my mother to thank her for carrying me. He was gone for many weeks, and my mother's breasts were not enough to feed me all by her lonesome. She had to squeeze the teat of our neighbor's goat, but the goat was inclined to dry up. I was born small and suckled little, and even now I only come up to my father's waist.

When my father returned to her, he got down on his knees and gave my mother a red fruit. He peeled away the leathery layer from one side, and there were thousands of dark seeds wrapped in paper-thin coverings, floating in rich juice. My mother held her hand open to receive it, and when my father gave it, the leather of the fruit grayed and hardened, the seeds burst in her hand, and it withered to half its size.

My mother ate one seed. She said it tasted like ash.

When I was older, I watched from my window the night my father went out alone with a small white candle. He kneeled before his fore-father's bent juniper and dug a shallow hole in the ground. He reached his left hand down to his thighs and trembled what lay between them, moaning all the while. When he sighed, he covered the hole and kneeled his lips to the ground and placed a kiss. He went inside with dirt on his face, and when I saw my mother in the morning there were dirt lips on her cheeks.

After, Father spent long months away from home, and during those months my mother stayed in the kitchen and smoked thin cigarettes. I asked her what was wrong, why didn't she move, but she only put her hand on my head and told me she was waiting for bad news, and that you must always wait for it in stillness, else it will arrive sooner than you like. When my father returned, he had a baby on his arm, fresh born, wrapped in white linen and with a diaper that smelled of rotting avo-cado. There was dirt on the babe's fingers and neck.

He needs changing, my father said to my mother. And milk.

Mother would not look at him.

When I reached to feel the baby's skin my father told me that the baby had been born of the tree outside—just like a miracle, this boy was!—and I was to love him as if he was my own brother, because he was, even if he really was not. He looked at my mother when he said this, though she would not look at him. She shook the ash off her cigarette.

Does the tree have a name? she asked him.

Father put his hand on my head and told me to go to my room. I did not move fast enough, and his thick fingers started to hurt, so I hid myself in the darkened corner of the living room. I am so small that I can hide in nearly any spot without being discovered, and so quiet that once I am out of sight I disappear.

Mother and Father stared at one another for a long time while my brother twittered on the table. It was strange, for surely they remem-bered what one another looked like, even after such a long separation.

Our son is hungry, my father said.

Is he? My mother asked. She did not move.

My father snapped the cigarette in her hand and drew her up. I curled down the wall when my father tore the dress from my mother's shoulders and squeezed her breast in his large hand. My own breasts, barely there, felt sick.

You think you'll find honey in stones? she hissed.

Father held my brother up to her chest and wrapped her arms around the boy. The filth dribbled out of his diaper where my father held him against her. When my brother put his lips on her breast my mother dripped and dripped and dripped, and she went pale and clenched her teeth.

In the morning the fruit my father had bought my mother was red, that deep red that is the ripe about to turn.

Every morning and midday and night I watch my mother unbutton the top of her dress and hold her breast to my baby brother. He used to push his little hands against her but now he only opens his mouth and lets his arms drop away with his fingers splayed. Young though he is, he understands that she does not like it when he touches her with anything other than his mouth. He is a very fat baby. His pink skin bunches in rolls around his creases. Mother has to hold him with both her arms.

My own arms are sticks and my legs little more than bone. Mother tells me I am beautiful, with skin as white as snow, hair as soft as a blackbird's wing, and when I cry and bite my lip, my mother says it is as bright as an opened tomato. As I grow, she tells me, I will be beautiful, and everyone will fall in love with me. My mother is kind, but I am old enough to know that I will no longer grow. I do not mind being small. I am quick if I do not run too long, and my fingers stretch and curve farther than my parents' can. When my brother's toys fall under the bed or under the cabinets, I am the only one who can retrieve them.

My brother cries, but not his usual soft twitter. He wails and screeches like the fox with its paw in a steel trap. My mother is no longer in the room, and I know she will not go to him, no matter how long or how hard he worries himself. I climb down from the tree and sneak past my mother, who is cutting tomatoes again, and go into my father's bedroom.

I coo and trace his faint blond eyebrows. He is such a beautiful, fat boy. Usually when I speak to him he will be silent and listen to me, but he only wails and wails, the baby bird fallen from his nest, sobbing for any mother. By his thigh under the blanket, his round, bulging thigh, I see a spot of red. My mother must have stained his blanket with the tomato.

Quiet now, I tell him. You mustn't carry on like this.

He cries until my father comes home, even though I have whispered every song and poem I know into his ear, and even though I conjure his future: that one day he will be a big boy, bigger than me, and we will play together under the tree where he was born.

I set the table for dinner—spoons and knives, for we are having soft bread and soup. My mother heated up the chopped tomatoes until they were soft and pulpy and stewed them in a broth with onion, and little sprigs of basil. She puts the old jar of salted berries I picked long ago on the table. My father and I greedily pile them onto the bottom of our bowl before my mother pours the soup. I dip the bread and chew.

It tastes tangy and sweet. I add more berries.

Mother eats only bread and watches my father as he darts out his tongue to lap up his bowl three times.

Best I've had, he says.

I'm glad, my mother says while chewing slowly. A drop on her bread is stained brownish-red. She must have cooked her tomatoes too long.

The wailing of my brother does not disturb either of them, but he is softer now, his yearning broken by exhaustion.

When it is dark, Father plants a big sloppy kiss on my cheek, which I think is too wet and wipe off. He laughs at me and flips my hair onto my face. I tell him to quit it, but I too am laughing and try to pull on the thin hairs at his arm, but even though my fingers are small, his hairs slip through my touch. Mother watches us and smokes.

I slump onto the couch. My father shakes his hips in front of my mother. He holds out his hand. She gives him hers. My belly happily gurgles and I feel drowsy, but I keep my eyes open to watch my parents dance around the small living room. Sometimes my father purposefully bumps into the couch or a table, and says, my oh my how clumsy I am. My mother laughs, real big kind of laughs, the kind you can't keep inside and don't want to anyway. He puts his hand on the small of her back.

When I open my eyes I am alone in the dark. My father's bedroom is open, and I can hear the faint whimpers of my brother. My father is not in his bed. My mother's door is closed. In the morning, my father is late to work.

The juniper tree has thick, rooty skin that has loosened with age, and I used to get small slivers of wood caught underneath the pink of my thumbs and fingers. Mother spent long hours tweezing them out and pressing down on the wound until it stopped bleeding. My hands are calloused now, too thick for the tree to crack through. No matter how much you love something, eventually you become thick to it.

My little brother sleeps, and when my mother goes into his room— there is no thunder in her legs today, she must be in a good mood— she stops and stares down at him. He coos, little sparrow boy, and she unbuttons her dress and lifts him to her breast.

At dinner that night my brother cries so loud in his room that my mother closes the door and shoves towels underneath to block the noise seeping out from the bottom. She serves my father and me pork cutlets, really juicy pink pieces, though small. She only eats bread and salad, and points to her waistline when my father asks her why she does not have any. My parents retire to my mother's room soon after the meal, after they bend down and push kisses onto either side of my face. I can hear them laughing.

I press my ear to my father's door. Behind, I hear my brother's wet breath, though he is quiet enough that I feel confident sneaking in. Brother is under a white sheet, it almost looks like a shroud, and if he were not wheezing I would have thought him dead. I peel the shroud away from his face. He looks up at me with his muddled blue eyes, the kind that my father said would eventually fade away into clear, but they never did. Brother scrunches his face into a prune, but I touch his lips and chin and he relaxes.

I tell him a story about a witch with a candy house in the middle of the forest, and how a brother and a sister, much like us, had thrown her into the oven, and baked her with pineapple juice and mint. They probably ate her, I tell him, else why go to so much trouble to prepare her?

I stay with him until he sleeps, and kiss his forehead. He tastes salty. I kiss him again. And again. I uncover his little toes, curled, and kiss those. Sweet. I lick them, then I cover him back up.

In the kitchen I warm up the leftovers from last night. At the top of the shelf where my mother put the fruit my father gave her, it has burst. Its insides drip over the edge of the shelf onto the floor. I wipe it up. The towel is stained.

My father is late again for work, and when he kisses me good-bye his mouth tastes like my mother's cigarettes. Mother shoos me outside, and I sit on the juniper tree and sing songs to myself. When my mother goes in to feed my brother, she sees me on the tree and waves. Then she closes the blinds, but I can still hear my brother wailing.

The house is quiet when I go back in. Mother is standing over a large pot on the stove, stirring with a wooden spoon. It smells delicious.

What are you making, I ask her.

Chili, she says. With beans and celery.

I make a face. I don't like celery.

You can pick it out, she tells me. I'll cook it so you cannot taste it. Don't be ungrateful.

Is brother sleeping? I ask her. I don't hear him.

She stops stirring and tells me to sit at the table. She brings me a piece of chocolate cake. She covers it in strawberry yogurt and puts it in front of me.

Don't tell your father, she says, and lights up a cigarette and sits beside me. It'll be our secret.

As I eat, she strokes my hair and tells me I am beautiful, the most beautiful child she has ever seen.

Darling, she tells me when I ask again about my brother. Don't you mind him. He is sleeping. You know I can't stand his screaming.

When he gets older he won't scream anymore, I tell her. You told me I stopped screaming young.

My mother stares at me in a queer sort of way. She says, You're a good girl. You knew better than to open your mouth.

But how else will Brother let us know he's unhappy? Or hungry. He can't walk yet.

She laughed at me. Darling, the unhappy don't scream. They fester and wait. They're very quiet people.

Can I help you with dinner? I ask.

Together, we cut the celery. I have to wipe my hands each time I lift them from the stalks. The smell makes me nauseous. Mother teaches me how to chop very fine, very carefully and slow, so that every piece comes out the same size, and you can barely tell there had been a cut at all.

She pulls out the meat, very fresh, very delicate, and teaches me how to cut it into small pieces.

Careful, Mother says. You have to leave the fat on. You're cutting too harsh. Use your fingers, like this, see?

I go to wash my fingers, but the red on my hands looks so sweet, I pop them into my mouth. Mother is watching me, strained. Then, she smiles.

It's OK, lovely girl. Sometimes you want things that are bad for you. Now, wash your hands. Use soap. Use lots of soap.

After, when all that is needed is heat and waiting, she tells me to go to my room and read. I take a collection of fables from my bookshelf. The house is quiet, so quiet. I prefer it when my brother is crying.

Before Father comes home, my mother takes a black, heavy bag and a shovel and goes to the Juniper tree. I watch her as she digs a hole near its base and dumps the bag in. She covers the hole with dirt and pounds it down with the back of the shovel.

Father comes home and picks me up and spins me around. I have never seen him so happy, and his happiness crawls onto me, and I laugh and laugh. He eats his chili with such force that his belly expands to twice his size, and he rubs it and belches. When he sees that my mother is not tasting her own food, he lifts up his spoon to her mouth, and she hesitates and then sticks out her tongue to taste. She grimaces and pulls back.

I made it too sweet, she says.

Mother tries to take my father into her room after the meal while I wash the dishes under the hot water, but he protests and says it is too far too walk, he feels so full, and his bedroom is closer.

We'll disturb the boy, she says, pulling on his arm.

He won't mind, my father says. Just like it used to be, you know?

My mother closes her eyes. She lifts up her chin and goes into his room. Father follows and closes the door behind him.

Before I finish the dishes, when my arms are deep in the pot trying to scrub off the sweet-burnt mess at the bottom, I hear my mother scream, and the sound of crashing.

Though I know I cannot be in trouble, I feel sick and hide behind the couch, peering over the edge as my father's door opens and my mother is tossed out so hard she slams against the hallway wall. Her body crumbles into itself. My father stands above her and clenches his fists again and again. She raises her head at him—her cheek red and her eyes wide—but he kicks her in her thigh, and she coughs and crumbles.

We have similar thighs, my mother and me. Small thighs—they do not touch—and when his foot and dirty toenails strike her I can feel it. I am from her belly, and in many ways her body is my own. I hate my father's toenails.

I'll ask you one more time, he tells her.

She moves slowly off the ground. Mother is small like me, especially when she stands next to my father. Like a leaf opening up to the light, she uncurls her body and stands on her shaking knees.

Where you got him from, she tells him. Every part of him.

My mother languishes on the floor where my father laid her low. I hear my father outside, wailing. I shake so hard my fingers rattle against each other. From the window, I see him clawing the dirt away from the juniper tree, making holes, until he drags the black bag up and clasps it to his chest.

He returns, the black bag tucked away under one of his arms. My mother is moaning on the floor by his bedroom. When he passes her it is if he cannot, or chooses not, to see her.

It'll just be us again, she sobs at him. We can turn back to how we used to be.

He steps on her ankle, and the sound of her bones cracking is louder than her yelp. She is so loud.

I hear my father weeping, but I only feel for my mother. Her hair, as dark as my own, is wet with sweat and matted against her forehead.

When I can move, and it is long before I can move, I wet a kitchen towel with cold water and place it against my mother's red face. She moans and tells me she loves me, and that it will all be OK soon enough.

It'll all go back to the way it was, she says. Bad things happen and they pass. Don't you worry, baby girl.

I can tell she believes it. I feel a sick kind of sorry for her, and then I feel a sick kind of sorry for myself, because I don't want to go back if that means we'll do this all over again. You can't take back what's already been bloomed.

She tries to stand but she is too heavy at her top, and her back is bent and all her hair and arms drag on the ground. She collapses and lies there outside Father's room. I put the towel under her head and kiss her and go to the kitchen.

I pick through the drawer where mother keeps all of the spatulas and wooden spoons and the extra knives she doesn't want me to touch because they are too heavy and too sharp. I take out the largest, the one she uses to chop up tomatoes, and carefully place it against my finger and slide it across. I lick the blood, and it tastes sweet. Too sweet. I must be candy inside, all sweetness.

The fruit my father gave my mother is no longer bleeding. I scramble up on the kitchen counter until I can reach it. It's stuck in its own juices and when I lift it, it leaves a piece of itself behind on the wood. It is gray again, hardened stone. I break off a seed and lift it to my mouth but it disintegrates away before I can put it on my tongue. I lick my fingers. Ash, just like my mother said. I climb down and throw it away. What a miserable present, one that dies and lives and dies again.

I am a small girl, and in the night my long hair covers the part of myself, my bright red lips, that I cannot keep silent or dark. I bite my hair. I creep quiet. My mother does not move when the floor slightly creaks under me and I stand still, watching her, making sure she does not waken.

When something dies, it should stay still. And it should never be allowed to hurt anyone again.

My father's door opens without noise, and though I do not know how he could be, my father is asleep in his bed, curled around the black bag. I look in the crib where my brother used to be and see only the white shroud, stained brown in places.

When you are small and quiet you can get anywhere you wish to be, and see anything you wish to see, though often you see exactly what you wish you would not. My feet, just skin covering tiny bones, barely makes an indention on the bed when I stand over him. Outside, the Juniper tree looks lonely and bare, only its bark visible, even though I know everything beautiful about it is still there, outside of my view, dragging on the ground. Why did my father never plant anything around it? Why did he leave it alone for so long?

I close my eyes and rest the knife along the soft indent of his throat. I count to three. I am weak, little girl weak, but even I am strong enough to get the knife down all the way to the bedcovers. He bleeds like the fruit he bought my mother, except worse. The fruit smelled like rot. He smells like salt metal.

Even a man without a throat can make a lot of noise. He opens his eyes and flails and gurgles and I know, when he saw me bent over on top of him, that he no longer thought me beautiful. I push the knife in deeper and he throws me off. I crash down to the ground, next to the black bag.

I saw Brother's fingers, little more than pink stubs poking out of that black nothingness. Mother must have drained him quite a bit. His skin is wrinkled, like a grandmother's, and at the tip of his pinky is a dollop of blood, just a drop, and I feel want in the back of my throat. I wait to see if he moves, but he no longer moves. Good, Brother, there is only suffering here.

I should have closed the door. My mother inches her way into the room at the noise and watches my father until he, too, is stillness. She calls his name. When he does not move, she whines his name like a bitch does for its master, that long pitiful whine. Then she sobs his name. The water slumps out of her eyes like big, fat mucous slugs. She beats her arms against the ground so hard she must be hurting herself, but she keeps doing it, and she keeps wetting her face, her clothes and her broken ankle.

Outside, the juniper tree began to uncurl its spine.

All who tremble

In a cold, gray city to the North there lived a family made of ragtag parts. The denizens all thought them strange, and when the towns-folk passed by the house the men and women pushed babushkas across and hats over their eyes to hide their faces from the windows. They plugged their ears with little blocks of wax when they passed, because there was a whirring from the basement that crawled up their bones and shook them until they were freezing. They always wore heavy wool coats as they passed to starve the chill as best they could.

The whirring, clunking buzz always emanated from the bottom of the house, no matter the time of day. The braver of the citizens com-plained about the noise in loud whispers from the street, but none dared complain near the door. There were stories of those who lived inside, a mother, her older daughter and young son, and the grandfather whom none had ever seen but whom everyone delighted in telling terrible stories about, but they were never entirely sure of any of them except the daughter, who bought cheese and bread and milk at the market, and who drank cold beer in the corner of the tavern. The brother and mother might be spied, sometimes, fluttering at the windows, moving too quickly to really see. When they asked the daughter about her family she gave them such an awful look that they felt their pricks and tits shrivel and dry up.

The problem, everyone agreed, was there was no father there. Some whispered he dallied off with a French actress he'd met in the service.

Other, kinder voices said he was still there on the property, his bones ground up and used as fertilizer for the half-grown flowers on the sill.

He isn't a particularly good fertilizer, they whispered to each other, safe and snide in their own homes. See how the petals wilt?

And that grandfather, they said to their children. He's terribly ugly. He has great big boils on his penis and eyebrows. If he touches you, you'll be ugly, too. No one will want to marry you.

Yet there were a few townsfolk to whom their wool coats had become as comfortable as their skin, and they stood in front of the house, shivering, sometimes crying, but always there. When asked why they did this, they said it was because they had grown used to the vibration, and did not know if they could live without it.

But it's horrible, people told them.

Yes, the wool coats said. It is.

* * *

The daughter of the whirring house kept her nose high and her skirts bunched up in her fists whenever she went out into the cold nights to make her money. She hadn't had the sense to be born beautiful, or even pretty, but her cheekbones were sharp enough to cut and her neck took to bruising well, and that fascinated the men who paid her for her time. When she came home to the whirring house she always had rubles and coins stuffed into the folds of her clothes and skin. These she meticulously pulled out to the last cent and dropped them on the kitchen table.

Her young brother, because he could not sleep, waited up for her every night and watched her release the money, his hands wrapped around a cold cup of water, his face wet and mucousy.

Keep crying, she said each night. Cry it all out, or the water in you will leak and you'll wet the bed again. Cry it out and go sleep.

I can't sleep, he said. The noise is keeping me up. It's whirly-burly.

Do you want me to go down and make it stop? she said. It was an old line between them. Once, when the old daughter was young, younger than her brother, she approached the basement door. As she drew nearer her body began to shake, her blood vibrated and grew hot to a boil. When she placed her open palm on the splintered wood she felt she would burst open. Afraid she would burn up, she drew her body away and went up onto the roof, as far away as she could be from the whir. She stayed up there all day. When she told her mother what she had felt when she touched the door, her mother slapped her across the face.

The brother sniffled. It's getting louder, he said, as he did each night. Will you sleep with me?

The old daughter shook her head and said, No, you're too old for that.

I'm only five, the young brother whined.

You've been five for six years, she reminded him. Tonight you will be six, and sleep alone.

But like every night the boy cried and cried until the old daughter crept into his bed and wrapped her arms around him and held him still. He did not sleep, but he quieted and wiped his face on her chest.

Poor brother, she said. And poor me. One day the whirring will make us all mad.

* * *

In the mornings, the mother separated the coins and rubles on the table into groups of like before bending over a pot of kasha and dropping in square slabs of margarine. None of them liked margarine, but honey and raisins were too expensive. They held their stomachs in until the grandfather plodded up the basement stairs on his three legs, one of which was sturdy and wooden and held tight in his withered hand. The old daughter held her breath when the basement door was open and the whirring was at its loudest. She kept her eyes on the table when her grandfather sat down, as he was ugly and it would have put her off breakfast.

I have a stomachache, said the daughter. She placed her spoon in the middle of her kasha to punctuate her point. It stood straight up.

The mother's spoon clattered to the floor. The young son sniffled.

It's the baby, said the daughter. I can feel him swimming in me. I'll have to get married, you know. I'll have a nice house with red table-cloths and a bird that sings commercials every morning and tells me what I deserve to own. I'll have a bright blue automobile with tinted windows so no one can look at me when I go out. My husband will cultivate earwax and he'll stuff it in my ears, but not before he tells me he loves he, and seals that promise in my head.

When no one said a word, she added, And I'll be happy, and there's nothing you can say against that.

The grandfather spooned up his kasha and put it in his slack and wet mouth. When he ate, no matter what it was, he always slurped.

The mother picked the spoon up from the floor held it to her son's face under his eyes. When he had cried enough on it she wiped it on her shirt and resumed eating.

But if you're happy, the mother asked calmly, how will we eat? Do you think your brother can work, with his condition? Don't be selfish. You're spectacular, little love. But you're only spectacular to us.

The grandfather stood and whacked his cane against the thin table legs. The old daughter watched the coins tremble and held her breath. The grandfather stood on his three legs and hobbled off to the basement. When the door was open she could hear the deep, hollow whir in her half empty stomach. She held her breath again. When it was closed it echoed miserably.

The children were naturally curious about their grandfather, but the mother had not offered to say much about him except that once he had been highly respected. He wore furs to the marketplace. Mink and red fox. And then, like all respected men, one day he was not, and went down into the basement. That was when the whirring started.

What does the whirring do? they asked.

It keeps away bad things, said the mother, touching her hair to make sure not a single strand had fallen out of place. It keeps us safe. If anyone goes down there but your grandfather, they'll change.

Change how?

Change, their mother said, cruel and final. And if I catch you, I'll beat you until you're numb.

Most days the old daughter did not care much for safety. She climbed up to the roof and she stretched out on the incline. There she recited all the things she knew for sure on her fingers: Change makes the sky burn all blue away to red. Permanent change occurs when the little bits inside of us go nutty with movement, heating up and deforming their shape until they cannot return to form. If you change too much you will fade away until only a shadow remains. Be careful of changing too much. She wanted to change very badly, she supposed.

When the sun was out she slept on the shaking shingles under her. Years of practice had cultivated a certain stillness in her slumber, so that she would not roll off the roof and break her neck. She would never voice it, but she was comforted, perhaps from custom if nothing else, by the way the house vibrated her bones, a mimicry of a rocking chair. When the stars were out she climbed back in and stood in front of her mirror for an hour, painting her lips and eyes and fitting a short dress around her breasts and hips. She kissed her sniveling brother on the head when he wrapped his limbs around her legs like a baby monkey and begged her to stay.

Can't you hear it getting louder? he said. It's going to eat me. I'm afraid it will stop.

You're not making any sense, she said. She shook her body to shove him off. She patted his head and said, I thought you wanted it to stop?

I don't know. I don't know. What if it's worse if it goes away?

Don't worry, she said. One day we will go far, far away from here.

Her brother sobbed and sobbed so loudly the old daughter had no choice but to abandon him and go outside. She ignored the men in wool coats who tipped their hats to her and called her ma'am, and went into the heart of the dank city, where she could breathe.

* * *

She went to the fanciest of the local bars—the one with eight bar-stools—and wrapped her arms around the current olive of her eye, a tall, lanky youth named Hiccup. He had dark eyes and worked in the bottle cap factory. He was the best man she'd ever been with; sometimes he brought her flowers with dirt clinging to their stems, and sometimes he would hold her afterwards, longer than anyone else had.

Baby, he said. Apple-baby-pie. You're my scrumptious buttonhole. You're dee-vine. Your nipples are like the biggest bottle caps I have ever seen and I've seen them all.

You're drunk, she said. Again. Then she laughed into his shoulder.

He fumbled for his wallet and pushed several crinkled bills between her breasts. His hand lingered and she let it linger. She pulled him to the back room where it was dark and none of the other drunk patrons could see her fall on him.

Try, she said. Really try this time. It has to take.

I am trying, he said, and rolled over onto his back.

Sure, she said. Yes. Then we'll have a country house, yes, won't we? A quiet home.

He grunted. She shifted her hips.

When they were done they sat at the bar and drank vodka on his dime. She liked to watch the way Hiccup threw his head back with each shot, the way his throat moved up and down when he swallowed, the little bit that would fall out of his thick lips and dribble down his chin. This was what she liked best about him.

* * *

Afterwards, and ever the gentleman, Hiccup took her to the Ferris wheel at the edge of town, the one in the amusement park that had not opened yet but, as Hiccup said, they could go now for free. Once it sparkled with lights and smiling children, that was the end of it. You'd have to pay to get in, and all the fun would disappear.

They climbed up the side of the wheel and sat in one of the carts halfway up. Hiccup threw his head back and exposed his throat, while the daughter rested her legs in his lap.

Look at the stars, he said. Pretty pretty lights.

She looked at the shapely ball in his throat and felt warmth spreading in her, like when Hiccup's paycheck came in and he could afford to buy an entire bottle of vodka, and he told her to take great big mouthfuls. But she had not drunk much this night, only the smallest bit, less than a cup, and only because Hiccup said he liked the way she moved when she did.

The warmth began in her belly, where their baby surely nestled this time, and rolled into her fingertips and into her knees, which, because they had never been so warm before, started to knock together. She could not sit still. She felt hot and happy and strange, and she so wanted Hiccup to feel as she did in this moment, though she had no words for him. Steadying herself against the cart, she leaned over to kiss him. As she did, she pictured him in the cozy home she dreamed of on the roof during the day with the sun basting her. He wore a top hat and a long coat, and he always, always smiled at her.

Oh bog, oh bog, said Hiccup. It's an earthquake.

What?

The Ferris wheel was shaking—she could see the metal buzz back and forth, and the ground looked blurry, but the daughter could not feel the movements of the wheel. To her, there was only movement, excitement, a life, contained in her body.

Don't you feel it? cried Hiccup. We're falling apart!

And they were: the wheel was vibrating, or maybe it was the earth beneath them knocking back and forth, but the wheel shook so hard the metal whined and bent. The daughter saw a screw near their car unwind and plink its way down to the ground.

It's going to crash down all around us! cried Hiccup.

She dug her hands into his arm. But we will be together, she said, desperate.

Hiccup grasped onto the side of the car, far away from her. We're going to die, he said. Oh, bog! I haven't drunk enough to die today!

She watched the fat tears trail down his face and felt the warmth in her core spread to her fingers, tingling there like it might shoot out of her in a burst of light and energy, and when she thought it could no longer remain with her, the warmth was gone.

It stopped, said Hiccup. Goodness.

The daughter wondered if it had happened at all. Hiccup's face was deluged with sweat, and though she cuddled into his chest, she could not help but think she was lying with her wet brother.

* * *

That night she came home happy, but her grandfather was waiting for her in the kitchen instead of her weepy brother. She looked at a point over her grandfather's head and crossed her arms. He did not speak.

I did it, she told him, delightfully vicious. I got pregnant tonight. It took. I know it. He loves me, too. She put her hands on the cage that cradled the new life and inched her fingers inside herself to grasp at the new, throbbing heart that must be there.

With effort the grandfather stood up, leaning on his cane. She shocked to a still statue when he put his withered arms around her. Her grandfather took a deep breath in and let it out in a low, high-pitched whine. His head shook against her breasts. She stared at his hairless, spotted crown. He was bumpy, like his bones were edging up out of his skin. He slipped down lower and wrapped his arms around her stomach. She pulled away but he held tight. She could feel his lumpy lips kissing her belly through her clothes. No matter how hard or what way she twisted he held on.

If there was anything alive inside the daughter it would have scurried away to avoid those lips, she knew that. Nothing moved, not even her blood. She wondered if there had been anything there, or if she was always as empty as she had ever been.

Her grandfather let go when she started to cry.

* * *

The daughter ran out into the night. It was cold, and she forgot her coat in her hurry, but she was happy to chill away the feeling of her grandfather's hot arms. She ran past the wool coats and she ran past the butcher's shop and the flower store with six pale, wilting roses in the window and all the way to Hiccup's house. She had never been inside, but once she had half-carried his heavy, drunk body to the stoop.

Hiccup, she cried, rapping her cold palms on the door. Please, please.

She could hear voices inside, twittering like birdcalls. Hiccup opened the door, his shirt unbuttoned.

Would you run away with me? she asked. Really, truly get out of here? Away from all these familiar things? I need to know.

His eyes rolled to the side, then back at her. Yeah, baby-girl, he said. But not tonight. I'm out of money. Aren't you cold? Let me get you a blanket.

He left. She heard soft voices from inside say, Is that the girl from the whirring house? I heard her whole family is mad.

And another: I live near them. I like the noise. It lulls me to sleep. What would our little city be without it?

And another: Have you seen their grandfather? He's an ugly old man. Crazy as a drowning cat, too. That madness passed down into the rest of them.

And another: They all vibrate like their house. She's the worst. No matter where she goes you can feel her coming.

A cold voice said: I hope she vibrates so hard she explodes.

Then they laughed.

Hiccup brought her a thick wool blanket and wrapped it around her. He rubbed her arms until her face was pink and asked her to go home.

* * *

When she came home her entire body was still. She had tied Hiccup's blanket around her neck like a cape to keep the chill out.

One of the wool coats outside her house grabbed her arm and held her.

Let go, she said.

The wool coat raised his head and sniffed. Something is different, he said. The other wool coats slowly moved around her, leaning into her, blocking her view of the house.

You feel different, another one said. Why?

Nothing has changed, she said, thinking they meant the non-baby in her belly. Now let me go.

They did not let go. They closed in on her, the wool of their coats scratched her cheeks and arms, and they kept asking, Why are you so still? Is it going to stop? Should we go home, now? What will we do?

The wool coats began to shake around her, and the more she pushed against them the harder they shook. They vibrated into blurs, and she heard their voices quiver in her ears: It's back, it's back! You've brought it back!

One, a smaller wool coat, shrilled, What will we do now that it is back?

She grunted and pushed at them. Leave me alone!

They fell around her like pins and lay on the ground. Big wool coats, with twitching feet sticking out the end.

* * *

She slammed the door to wake up her mother, who came to the top of the stairs in her thin, white nightgown and shook the wooden curlers in her hair. Her brother came out of the kitchen, his eyelids fluttering, a cold cup of water sloshing with his dizzy steps.

The daughter held her empty belly in one hand and made a fist with the other. She strode toward the basement door with her teeth bared.

What are you doing? the mother asked, then she clenched her bony fists and said, Don't you dare, when the daughter reached for the door handle. You come back here, you horrible thing!

No, said the old daughter. I'm going to see what's down there.

The mother screeched and grabbed onto the ends of the blanket and pulled back while the daughter leaned forward and choked. Her brother dropped his water and sobbed.

No, don't, he cried. What if it is worse if it is gone? He wrapped himself around his sister's legs. When she tried to disentangle his weak body she fell and her family came toppling down.

Her mother jumped on top of her and wrapped her fingers around her daughter's neck. The wooden rollers in her hair began to fall out, leaving soft curls behind.

It's just until you calm down, the mother said, squeezing. Then I'll stop and we'll have some kasha like a family should.

But her mother was feeble. The daughter brought up her fist and socked her mother in the jaw. The mother fell to the floor. All her wooden rollers fell away, but when the daughter put her hand on her mother's face to hold her down, her curls shuddered and straightened out.

The daughter looked at her brother's wet face and said, Little darling, didn't you want it to change?

Please, he said. I'm used to this. No, I don't know. No. I'll be six if you want, if you really want.

But he was so tired and woozy that when she gently pushed him over he landed on his back with a sigh.

The daughter clambered to her feet and stood in front of the basement door. The doorknob was hot under her hand and she cringed. Once she turned it, she knew, as she knew the things she could count on her hand, whatever was behind the door would change everything.

The knob creaked.

I'll never forgive you! her mother said, holding her sobbing son in her arms. You're dead to us, do you hear me? Dead if you go down there!

Beyond the basement door the whirring was so loud the daughter could feel it bombinate in her blood and marrow, and she could almost convince herself that the movement was something alive inside her. Something electrified. With each step she descended the thrum in her grew until it was so frenzied it was hard to remember herself as whole; she felt like she was everywhere. It hurt and it was so good. The plaster and wood of the house trembled beneath her, but nothing quaked as greatly as her body. Her skin pulled away, stretched thin and taut. She was beaten upon by the whir and her skin beat back. There was so much wonderful whizzing and whirring inside of her, how had she never noticed?

When she finally arrived, would her body detonate in a flash and spread across the whole city in a brief but enduring stain on their storefronts, their wombs, their memory, or would she be a dud and fade away?

Acknowledgments

Many people have supported this work through encouragement, revision comments, writing sessions, the occasional sad alcoholic beverage, and endless compassion for weird stories. I would like to thank the women and men who have mentored me, especially William Jablonsky, James Pollock, Lawrence Coates, Wendell Mayo, Michael Czyzniejewski, Marly Swick, Trudy Lewis, Elaine Lawless, Carsten Strathausen, Maureen Stanton and Alexandra Socarides. Special, loving thanks to the women who wrote with me, read my work far too many times, rejoiced with me in success and comforted me in disappointment, especially Misha Rai, Michelle Zuppa, Colette Arrand, Karen Craigo and LaTanya McQueen. Thank you to my long-suffering friends, who occasionally inspired the work but mostly were emotional cornerstones: Beth Gorski, Carla Mazighi and Sarah Landolfi. Thank you for all the times you made me laugh, and more so for the times you made me think. Thanks especially to my husband, Nathan Riggs who sat with me on far too many stoops listening to my ideas for these stories. Thank you, Angela Carter, for existing once upon a time, and leaving me stories that still cut me and open me up and make me hope for something wonderful. Thank you Emily St. John Mandel for choosing this collection out of so many, and thank you to Andrew Gifford and everyone at Santa Fe Writers Project for giving this work a home.

Thank you to the editors and literary magazines who published these stories in slightly altered versions first:

Sequestrum: "Put Back Together Again"
Apex Magazine: "All Who Tremble"
The SouthEast Review: "Postpartum"
The Madison Review: "Eden"

Shimmer: "Food My Father Feeds Me, Love My Husband Shows Me"
Kill Author: "The Romantic Agony of Lemonhead"
Vestal Review: "Mermaid"
A Capella Zoo: "Three Times Red"
Children Churches and Daddies: "Beasts"
Gargoyle: "The Ibex Girl of Qumran"
Permafrost: "Suburban Alchemy"
Deathless Press: "Let Down Your Long Hair and then Yourself"
Kendall Hunt Publishing: "Juniper"

At the end, however, thank you most of all to my parents, Ken and Judy, who always supported my writing even though it was not always the most sensible choice. Thank you to my mother, who read the entire *Chronicles of Narnia* aloud to me while I was sick as a child, for giving me a love of words and a love of fantastical stories. Thank you also to my father, who took me to a book store and purchased *The Odyssey* when I was eight years old, proudly telling the seller that the book was not for him, but for the awkward child next to him who really wanted to read it. In retrospect, it was probably not age appropriate reading, but I thank you for not questioning that. Thank you for encouraging me to do this. And thank you both for shaping me into who I am.

About the Author

Angela Wood

A.A. Balaskovits is the winner of the Santa Fe Writers Project 2015 Literary Awards Program. Her fiction and essays have been published in numerous journals and magazines, including *Indiana Review, The Madison Review, Gargoyle, The Southeast Review* and *Apex Magazine.* She is the winner of the 2015 New Writers Award from Sequestrum. She holds a Ph.D. in English from the University of Missouri and an MFA from Bowling Green State University. Originally from the Chicagoland area, she now resides in South Carolina. *Magic for Unlucky Girls* is her first book.

www.aabalaskovits.com

Also from Santa Fe Writers Project

Bystanders *by Tara Laskowski*

"'Short story' and 'thriller' tend to be incompatible genres, but not in the hands of Tara Laskowski. BYSTANDERS is a bold, riveting mash-up of Hitchcockian suspense and campfire-tale chills."
— Jennifer Egan, author of
A Visit from the Goon Squad and *The Keep*

Modern Manners for Your Inner Demons
by Tara Laskowski

Blending humor with a sharp social commentary, Laskowski introduces us to cynical yet sympathetic characters as each story unfolds. These characters are the folks you want sitting next to you at your next dinner party...or in your prison cell.

The Poor Children *by April L. Ford*

Ford explores the eccentric, the perverse, the disenfranchised, and the darkly comic possibilities at play in us all.

"From the amazing first sentence of April L. Ford's debut collection, The Poor Children, *I was hooked. This is a rarity: a compellingly original voice and vision."*
— David Morrell,
New York Times *bestselling author*

About Santa Fe Writers Project

SFWP is an independent press founded in 1998 that embraces a mission of artistic preservation, recognizing exciting new authors, and bringing out of print work back to the shelves.

Find us on Facebook, Twitter @sfwp, and at www.sfwp.com $\text{s}f\mathbf{WP})$